THE PERFECT PARAGON

THE PERFECT PARAGON

An Agatha Raisin Mystery

M. C. BEATON

THORNDIKE
CHIVERS

This Large Print edition is published by Thorndike Press®, Waterville, Maine USA and by BBC Audiobooks Ltd, Bath, England.

Published in 2005 in the U.S. by arrangement with St. Martin's Press, LLC.

Published in 2006 in the U.K. by arrangement with Constable & Robinson Ltd.

U.S. Hardcover 0-7862-8004-2 (Mystery)
U.K. Hardcover 1-4056-3642-4 (Chivers Large Print)
U.K. Softcover 1-4056-3643-2 (Camden Large Print)

The text of this Large Print edition is unabridged.
Other aspects of the book may vary from the original edition.

Set in 16 pt. Plantin by Minnie B. Raven.

Printed in the United States on permanent paper.

British Library Cataloguing-in-Publication Data available

Library of Congress Cataloging-in-Publication Data

Beaton, M. C.
    The perfect paragon : an Agatha Raisin mystery / by M. C. Beaton.
        p. cm. — (Thorndike Press large print mystery)
    ISBN 0-7862-8004-2 (lg. print : hc : alk. paper)
        1. Raisin, Agatha (Fictitious character) — Fiction.
2. Women private investigators — England — Cotswold Hills — Fiction.   3. Husbands — Crimes against — Fiction.   4. Inheritance and succession — Fiction.
5. Cotswold Hills (England) — Fiction.   6. Widows — Fiction.   7. Large type books.   I. Title.   II. Series: Thorndike Press large print mystery series.
PR6052.E196P47 2005b
    823'.914—dc22   2005016837

This book is dedicated to
Dawn and Clive Simons
and their daughters,
Keriann and Kimberlee,
with affection.

One

Everyone in the village of Carsely in the English Cotswolds was agreed on one thing — no one had ever seen such a spring before.

Mrs. Bloxby, the vicar's wife, stepped out into her garden and took a deep breath of fresh-scented air. Never had there been so much blossom. The lilac trees were bent down under the weight of purple and white blooms. White hawthorn hedges formed bridal alleys out of the country lanes. Clematis spilled over walls like flowery waterfalls, and wisteria decorated the golden stone of the cottages with showers of delicate purple blooms. All the trees were covered in bright, fresh green. It was as if the countryside were clothed like an animal in a deep, rich pelt of leaves and flowers.

The few misery-guts in the village shook their heads and said it heralded a harsh winter to come. Nature moved in a mysterious way to protect itself.

The vicarage doorbell rang and Mrs.

Bloxby went to answer it. Agatha Raisin stood there, stocky and truculent, a line of worry between her eyes.

"Come in," said Mrs. Bloxby. "Why aren't you at the office? No cases to solve?"

Agatha ran her own detective agency in Mircester. She was well dressed, as she usually was these days, in a linen trouser suit, and her glossy brown hair was cut in a fashionable crop. But her small brown eyes looked worried.

Mrs. Bloxby led the way into the garden. "Coffee?"

"No," said Agatha. "I've been drinking gallons of the stuff. Just wanted a chat."

"Chat away."

Agatha felt a sense of comfort stealing over her. Mrs. Bloxby with her mild eyes and grey hair always had a tranquillizing effect on her.

"I could do with a really big case. Everything seems to be itty-bitty things like lost cats and dogs. I don't want to run into the red. Miss Simms, who was acting as secretary, has gone off with my full-time detective, Patrick Mulligan. He's retired and doesn't want to be bothered any more with work. Sammy Allen did the photo work, and Douglas Ballantyne the technical stuff. But I had to let them go. There just wasn't enough work. Then Sally Fleming, who replaced Patrick, got lured away by a London detective agency, and my treasure of a secretary, Mrs. Edie Frint, got married again.

"Maybe the trouble was that I gave up taking divorce cases. The lawyers used to put a good bit of business my way."

Mrs. Bloxby was well aware that Agatha was divorced from the love of her life, James Lacey, and thought that was probably why Agatha did not want to handle divorce cases.

She said, "Maybe you should take on a few divorce cases just to get the money rolling again. You surely don't want any murders."

"I'd rather have a murder than a divorce," muttered Agatha.

"Perhaps you have been working too hard. Maybe you should take a few days off. I mean, it is a glorious spring."

"Is it?" Agatha gazed around the glory of the garden with city eyes which had never become used to the countryside. She had sold up a successful public relations company in London and had taken early retirement. Living in the Cotswolds had been a dream since childhood, but Agatha still carried the city, with all its bustle and hectic pace, inside herself.

"Who have you got to replace Patrick and Miss Simms? Are you sure you wouldn't like anything? I have some home-made scones."

Agatha was tempted, but the waistband of her trousers was already tight. She shook her head. "Let me see . . . staff. Well, there's a Mrs. Helen Freedman from Evesham as secretary. Middle-aged, competent, quite a treasure. I do all the detecting myself."

"And for the technical and photographic stuff?"

"I'm looking for someone. Experts charge so much."

"There's Mr. Witherspoon in the village. He's an expert cameraman and so good with computers and things."

"I know Mr. Witherspoon. He must be about a hundred."

"Come now. He's only seventy-six and that's quite young these days."

"It's not young. Come on. Seventy-six is creaking."

"Why not go and see him? He lives in Rose Cottage by the school."

"No."

Mrs. Bloxby's normally mild eyes hardened a fraction. Agatha said hurriedly, "On

10

the other hand, it wouldn't hurt me to go along for a chat." Agatha Raisin, who could face up to most of the world, crumpled before the slightest suggestion of the vicar's wife's displeasure.

Rose Cottage, despite its name, did not boast any roses. The front garden had been covered in tarmac to allow Mr. Witherspoon to park his old Ford off the road. His cottage was one of the few modern ones in Carsely, an ugly redbrick two-storeyed affair. Agatha, who knew Mr. Witherspoon only by sight, was prepared to dislike someone who appeared to have so little taste.

She raised her hand to ring the doorbell but it was opened and Mr. Witherspoon stood there. "Come to offer me a job?" he said cheerfully.

Much as she loved Mrs. Bloxby, in that moment Agatha felt she could have strangled her. She hated being manipulated and Mrs. Bloxby appeared to have done just that.

"I don't know," said Agatha gruffly. "Can I come in?"

"By all means. I've just made coffee."

She telephoned him as soon as I left. That's it, thought Agatha. She followed him into a room made into an office.

It was impeccably clean and ordered. A computer desk stood at the window flanked on either side with shelves of files. A small round table and two chairs dominated the centre of the room. On the wall opposite the window were ranks of shelves containing a collection of cameras and lenses.

"Sit down, please," said Mr. Witherspoon. "I'll bring coffee."

He was an average-sized man with thick grey hair. His face was not so much lined as crumpled, as if one only had to take a hot iron to it to restore it to its former youth. He was slim.

No paunch, thought Agatha. At least he can't be a boozer.

He came back in a short time carrying a tray with the coffee things and a plate of scones.

"Black, please," said Agatha. "May I smoke?"

"Go ahead."

Well, one good mark so far, thought Agatha. "I'll get you an ashtray," he said. "Have a scone."

When he was out of the room, Agatha stared at the plate of scones in sudden suspicion. She picked up one and bit into it.

12

Mrs. Bloxby's scones. She would swear to it. Once again, she felt manipulated and then experienced a surge of malicious glee at the thought of turning him down.

He came back and placed a large glass ashtray next to Agatha.

He sat down opposite her and said, "What can I do for you?"

"Just a social call," said Agatha.

A flicker of disappointment crossed his faded green eyes.

"How nice. How's the detective business?"

"Not much work at the moment."

"That's odd. There's so much infidelity in the Cotswolds, I would have thought you would have enough to keep you busy."

"I don't do divorce cases any more."

"Pity. That's where the money is. Now, take Robert Smedley over in Ancombe. He's very rich. Electronics company. Madly jealous. Thinks his wife is cheating on him. Pay anything to find out."

They studied each other for a long moment. I really need the money, thought Agatha.

"But he hasn't approached me," she said at last.

"I could get him to."

Agatha had a sizeable bank balance and

stocks and shares. But she did not want to become one of those sad people whose life-time savings were eaten up by trying to run an unsuccessful business.

She said tentatively. "I need someone to do bugging and camera work."

"I could do that."

"It sometimes means long hours."

"I'm fit."

"Let me see, this is Sunday. If you could have a word with this Mr. Smedley and bring him along to the office tomorrow, I'll get my Mrs. Freedman to draw you up a contract. Shall we say a month's trial?"

"Very well, you won't be disappointed."

Agatha rose to her feet and as a parting shot said, "Don't forget to thank Mrs. Bloxby for the scones."

Outside, realizing she had forgotten to smoke, she lit up a cigarette. That was the trouble with all these anti-smoking people around these days. It was almost as if their disapproval polluted the very air and forced one to light up when one didn't want to.

Because of the traditions of the Carsely Ladies' Society, women in the village called each other by their second names.

So Mrs. Freedman was Mrs. Freedman even in the office, but Mr. Witherspoon volunteered his name was Phil.

Agatha was irritated when Phil turned up alone, but he said that Robert Smedley would be along later. After he didn't protest at the modest wages Agatha was offering him, she felt guilty and promised him more if his work should prove satisfactory.

The office consisted of one low-beamed room above a shop in the old part of Mircester near the abbey. Agatha and Mrs. Freedman both had desks at the window: Phil was given Patrick's old desk against the wall. There was a chintz-covered sofa and a low coffee table flanked by two armchairs for visitors. Filing cabinets and a kettle on a tray with a packet of tea and a jar of instant coffee, milk and sugar cubes made up the rest of the furnishings.

Mr. Robert Smedley arrived at last and Agatha's heart sank. He looked the sort of man she heartily despised. First of all, he was crammed into a tight suit. It had originally been an expensive one and Mr. Smedley was obviously of the type who would not admit to putting on weight or to spending money to have the suit altered. He had small black eyes in a doughy face shadowed by bushy black eyebrows. His flat head of hair was jet-black. Hair dyes are getting better these days, thought Agatha. Almost looks real. He had a small pursed mouth, "like an arsehole," as Agatha said later to Mrs. Bloxby, and then had to apologize for her bad language.

"Please sit down," said Agatha, mentally preparing to sock him with a large fee and get rid of him. "How may I be of help?"

"This is very embarrassing." Mr. Smedley glared round the small office. "Oh, very well. I think Mabel is seeing another man."

"Mabel being your wife?" prompted Agatha.

"Yes."

"What makes you think she might be having an affair?"

"Oh, little things. I came home early one day and I heard her singing."

"Why is that so odd?"

"She never sings when I'm around."

Can't blame her for that, thought Agatha sourly.

"Anything else?"

"Last week she bought a new dress without consulting me."

"Women do that," said Agatha patiently. "I mean, why would she need your permission to buy a new dress?"

"I choose all her clothes. I'm an important man and I like to see my wife dressed accordingly."

"Anything else?"

"Isn't that enough? I tell you, if she's seeing someone I want evidence for a divorce."

In that moment Agatha could have strangled both Phil and Mrs. Bloxby. She had been inveigled into hiring a geriatric all on the promise of this case and now it seemed that Smedley was nothing more than a jealous bully.

So in order to get rid of him, she named a very heavy fee and expenses. He took out his chequebook. "I'll give you a thousand pounds down and you can bill me for the expenses and for the rest if you are successful."

Agatha blinked rapidly, thought of her overheads, and accepted the cheque.

When Robert Smedley had left, Agatha said crossly to Phil, "This is all a load of rubbish, but we may as well make the moves. You and I will go over to Ancombe and stake out the house. Have you got your camera?"

"Got a car full of them," said Phil cheerfully.

17

"Okay, let's go."

Ancombe was only a few miles from Carsely. They quickly found Smedley's home. It was on the outskirts of the village in a heavily wooded area, perched on a rise. It had originally been a small eighteenth-century cottage built of the local mellow golden stone, but a large extension had been added to the back. Phil parked his car a little way away off the road in the shelter of a stand of trees. He took out a camera with a long telescopic lens.

"I'm slipping," mourned Agatha. "I should have asked him for a photograph of her."

Phil peered down the road. "There's a car just coming out of the driveway. Here, you take the wheel. We'll follow."

Agatha swung the wheel and followed at a discreet distance while Phil photographed the car and the number plate.

"She's heading for Moreton," said Agatha. "Probably going to buy another dress or something evil like that."

"She's turning into the station," said Phil. "Maybe going to meet someone."

"Or take the train," said Agatha.

A small, dowdy-looking woman got out of the car. "I hope that's her and not the cleaner," said Agatha. "If he chose that dress for her, he should be shot."

Who they hoped was Mabel Smedley was wearing a cotton shirtwaister in an eye-watering print. The hem practically reached her ankles and she was wearing patent leather shoes with low heels. She had dusty, sandy hair pulled back in a bun. She was obviously much younger than her husband. Smedley, Agatha guessed, looked around late forties. If this was Mrs. Smedley, she looked in her early thirties. Her face, devoid of make-up, was unlined and with no outstanding features. Small tired eyes, regular mouth, small chin.

She turned into the ticket office. As usual, there was a queue, so they were able to stand a few people behind her. They heard her order a day return to Oxford.

When it came their turn, they asked for day returns as well and then went over the bridge to the platform.

Phil had unscrewed the telescopic lens and snapped several discreet shots of Mrs. Smedley waiting for the train.

The train was ten minutes late in that usual irritating way of trains — like some boss keeping you waiting ten minutes outside his door to stress what a busy and important man he was.

She got out at Oxford and began to

walk. They followed. Agatha took out her mobile phone and called Mrs. Bloxby. "Do you know what Mrs. Smedley looks like?"

"Yes, you must have seen her before, Mrs. Raisin, but maybe you didn't notice her. She does a lot of work for the Ancombe Ladies' Society. She's small and thin with sandy hair. I think she's about fourteen years younger than her husband. Very quiet. What . . . ?"

"Tell you later," said Agatha and rang off. "That's her, all right," she said to Phil. "Wonder where she's going?"

They followed her along Worcester Street and then along Walton Street. At last, Mrs. Smedley stopped outside the Phoenix Cinema and went in.

"Don't get too caught up in the film," hissed Agatha.

They bought tickets. The cinema was nearly empty. They took seats three rows behind her. The film was a Russian one called *The Steppes of Freedom.* It was beautifully photographed, but to Agatha's jaundiced eyes, nothing seemed to happen apart from the heroine either bursting into tears or staring out across the steppes. Obviously Mrs. Smedley was as bored as Agatha because, before the end, she got up. They gave her a few minutes before following. Back along Walton Street and so down to the station.

Back on the train to Moreton and from there they followed her home.

"Maybe she hoped to meet someone," said Phil, "and he didn't turn up. I mean, it seems odd to go all that way to sit through a dreary film."

"You got photos of her going into the cinema?"

"Of course."

"I know," said Agatha. "Let's go and see Mrs. Bloxby. She seems to know all about Mrs. Smedley."

They drove to the vicarage. Alf Bloxby, the vicar, answered the door and his face hardened into displeasure when he saw Agatha.

"If you've come to see my wife, she's busy," he said.

Mrs. Bloxby appeared behind him. "What are you talking about, Alf? Do come in, Mrs. Raisin. And Mr. Witherspoon, too."

The vicar muttered something like *pah* under his breath and strode off to his study.

"Let's go into the garden," said Mrs. Bloxby. "Such a fine day. It won't last, of course. As soon as Wimbledon comes around, then the rain comes down again."

They sat at a table in the garden. "I see you've employed Mr. Witherspoon," said Mrs. Bloxby brightly.

"For the moment," retorted Agatha. "He's on trial. The case we're on involves Mrs. Mabel Smedley. Her husband thinks she's having an affair."

"That doesn't seem very likely. I mean, a small place like Ancombe. Such news would soon get out."

"What's she like?"

"Hard to tell. Have you forgotten, Mrs. Raisin? The Ancombe Ladies' Society is having a sale of work the day after tomorrow and some of us are going over to help. You could come along and see for yourself. Mrs. Smedley works very hard for good causes, but she is quiet and self-effacing. They've only been married for two years."

"Any children?"

"No, and none by Mr. Smedley's first marriage either."

"What happened to the first Mrs. Smedley?"

"Poor thing. She was subject to bouts of depression. She committed suicide."

"I'm not surprised. Married to a creature like that." Agatha described him in trenchant terms, ending up with that description of his mouth.

"Mrs. Raisin! Really."

"Sorry," mumbled Agatha.

Phil stifled a laugh by pretending he had a sneezing fit.

"I think Mr. Smedley is just unnaturally jealous," said Mrs. Bloxby.

"Oh dear," sighed Agatha. "It all seems such a waste of time. We'll leave it for today, Phil, and you can drive me back to the office so I can collect my car. I'll see you in the office tomorrow. I've a few things to work on."

Just as Agatha was setting down to a dinner of microwaved chips and microwaved lasagne that evening, the telephone rang. "Don't dare touch my food," she warned her cats, Hodge and Boswell.

She answered the phone and heard the slightly camp voice of her former assistant, Roy Silver.

"I haven't heard from you in ages," he said. "No more killings down there?"

"No, nothing. Just a divorce case and I hate divorce cases."

"Stands to reason, sweetie. You being such a reluctantly divorced woman yourself."

"That is not the reason! I just find them distasteful."

"Divorce cases are surely the bread and butter of any detective agency. Why I'm phoning is to ask you if I can come down for the weekend."

"Next weekend? All right. Let me know which train you'll be on and I'll meet you at Moreton."

When Agatha rang off, she felt cheerful at the thought of having company. She had endured a brief unhappy marriage to James Lacey. They hadn't even lived in the same house. But after it was over, she found herself getting lonely when she wasn't working full out.

Then Agatha realized she hadn't tackled Mrs. Bloxby over manipulating her into employing Phil. She rang up the vicar's wife.

"Mrs. Bloxby," began Agatha, "I feel you forced me into employing Phil."

"Mr. Witherspoon. I suppose I did push you in that direction."

"Why? You're not a pushy woman."

Mrs. Bloxby sighed. "I happened to learn that he has only a small pension. He made some bad investments with his capital. He is desperately in need of money and was ready to sell off some of his precious cameras. You needed a photographer, he needed work. I couldn't help myself."

"Oh, well," muttered Agatha, somewhat mollified. "We'll see how he works out."

"Going to Ancombe?"

"Of course. I forgot to ask you what time it begins."

"Two in the afternoon."

"I'll be there."

Agatha returned to the kitchen to find her cats up on the table, tucking in to her dinner. "You little bastards," she howled. She opened the kitchen door and shooed them both out into the garden. She scraped her dinner into the rubbish bin and suddenly burst into tears.

She finally mopped her eyes on a dish-cloth and lit a cigarette with a trembling hand. Agatha was in her early fifties, but recently had been assailed with a fear of getting old and living alone. On damp days, she had a stabbing pain in her hip but stoically ignored it. She couldn't possibly have arthritis. She was too young!

"Pull yourself together," she said aloud. Was this the menopause at last? She had been secretly proud of the fact that she had not yet reached that borderline.

The phone rang again. Agatha wearily went to answer it.

"Charles, here."

Agatha's friend, Sir Charles Fraith.

"Oh, hullo, Charles. Where have you been lately?" Agatha gave a gulping sob.

"Have you been crying, Aggie?"

"Don't call me Aggie. Bit of an allergy, that's all."

"Have you eaten?"

"I was about to but the cats got to it."

"I'll be right over. I was to entertain some luscious girl to a picnic and she never showed. I'll bring it right over and we'll have a picnic in your garden."

"Oh, thanks, Charles."

"So dry your eyes."

"I haven't been crying!" But Charles had rung off.

He turned up half an hour later, which had given Agatha time to bathe her face in cold water and put on fresh make-up.

She was glad to see Charles, even though she occasionally found him irritating. He had fair hair and neat features and was as self-contained and independent as a cat.

He carried a large hamper into the garden and began to set things out on the garden table.

"Duck breasts in aspic, asparagus, champagne . . . you really must have thought a lot of this girl."

26

"She is very ornamental," said Charles. "Unfortunately for me, she knows it."

They ate companionably while Agatha told him about the Smedley case.

"Might go with you," said Charles. "Mind if I stay the night?"

"No, you know where the spare room is."

"I've got my bag in the car. I'll get it later."

The sun slowly set behind the trees at the bottom of the garden. Agatha thought uneasily about her burst of tears. It all seemed like madness now.

Two

Charles was still in bed the following morning when Agatha set out for the office fortified with a breakfast of two cigarettes and a cup of black coffee.

"What have we got today?" she asked Mrs. Freedman.

"Still got that missing-teenager case, one missing dog and one missing cat."

"Peanuts," said Agatha gloomily. "I've got the morning free, so I may as well get back out there looking for them. We'll leave Mabel Smedley for now."

"I'll come with you," volunteered Phil.

"Oh, all right," said Agatha. "We'll start with the teenager, Jessica Bradley."

"That's been in all the papers," said Phil. "Left the Happy Night Club at one in the morning and just disappeared. The police haven't been able to find a trace of her."

"I've interviewed the people who run the club," said Agatha, "and her friends. She left alone. Doesn't seem to have a boyfriend. I don't know what we can find out that the police can't."

"Perhaps," suggested Phil, "we could walk from the club to her home, just to get a feel of the area."

"I've done that," snapped Agatha. "The police have even had a look-alike on television doing that."

"Sometimes people try so hard, they're not really looking," said Phil. "Wouldn't hurt just to take the walk again."

"Oh, well," sighed Agatha. "It's better than sitting here. Give me her photo and those cat and dog photos, Mrs. Freedman. Who knows? We might get lucky and find one of them in the street."

They made their way to the Happy Night Club. It was in a dingy backstreet.

"It's quite a walk," said Agatha.

"As far as I remember," said Phil, "she lives in Old Brewery Road out by the bypass."

"Right. I don't know what you hope to achieve by this walk, but I'm prepared to try anything."

The day was becoming quite hot. Agatha had put on a pair of high-heeled sandals that morning and her feet were beginning to ache. The houses began to thin out as they approached the bypass. "We take the bridge over the bypass," said Agatha.

As they reached the centre of the bridge, Phil said, "Stop!"

"What?"

"Just want to look. How long's she been missing?"

"Three days."

"How old is she?"

"Sixteen."

Phil was carrying his camera bag. He knelt down and opened it and took out a camera and a telescopic lens.

"Going to photograph the bypass?"

"Sometimes I can see things with this that other people miss."

Normally Agatha would have protested, but it was a relief to stop walking and ease her feet.

"It's a high climb up to the bridge," said Phil after what seemed like an age, "and there wouldn't be much traffic on the bypass at that time of night. Now, if I were Jessica, I wouldn't bother climbing the bridge, I'd nip across the dual carriageway. So say she's standing over there waiting to cross and a car pulls up."

"I don't think any teenager is going to get into a strange car in the middle of the night."

"True. But what if it were someone she knew?"

"So, Sherlock, we're worse off than ever. She gets in the car, is driven off and could be anywhere in England."

"Tell me about her parents."

"Then let's get back off this bridge. I'm frying up here. There's a nice bit of shade in the grass on the other side."

They walked over and climbed up a grassy bank. "Father, Frank Bradley, works in an ice cream factory. Forties. Cut up about his daughter. Wife about the same age. Tired-looking, cries the whole time."

"What were they about, letting Jessica stay out so late? I mean, she's only sixteen."

"They had told her to be home by eleven. When she didn't show, the father went out looking for her."

"What if the father *did* find her? What if she got in the car and he lost his temper and she cheeked him and he thumped her too hard? Have the police looked closely at the family?"

"Yes. First thing they thought of."

"Okay." Phil's eyes looked oddly young in his wrinkled face. "But they wouldn't make any particular push. Grieving parents and all that."

"I thought of the father right off as well as the police," said Agatha. "But I'd swear

31

to God the man is genuine."

"What about uncles? Neighbours?"

"I don't know," said Agatha crossly.

"You know, we could go back and get the car and pretend that she was picked up and drive along the dual carriageway and see if there's anywhere to dump a body. The police can't search everywhere."

"I'm the detective, not you," snapped Agatha. Phil looked at her mournfully.

"It's the heat," said Agatha by way of apology. "Look, my feet hurt. Be an angel and get the car and I'll wait here."

"Righto," said Phil cheerfully. "Watch my cameras and I'll be back in a tick."

He strode off. I think he's fitter than me, thought Agatha. Her hip gave a nasty little twinge and she rubbed it fiercely.

Phil was soon back. Agatha crossed back over the bridge and got into his car. "No air conditioning," she moaned.

"If you open the window you'll get a nice breeze," said Phil.

Agatha opened the window and a hot dry wind sent her hair whipping about her face. She shut it partly. "How far are we going?" Phil was cruising along slowly, looking carefully to left and right.

"I'm thinking. You think, too, Mrs. Raisin. I am an uncle, say, or neighbour.

Jessica starts to complain, 'This isn't the road home.' He can't go on much further without making some sort of attack. Ten miles, I'd say."

Agatha closed her eyes and tried to imagine the scene. If it were someone Jessica knew well, she'd be chattering happily. They would be on the wrong side of the dual carriageway for home, so at first she wouldn't notice anything until they came to the first roundabout and realized he hadn't turned round to go back.

She opened her eyes. "Try three miles after the first roundabout."

Phil went across the first roundabout and slowed down to a crawl as other cars passed him at speed. At last he pulled over into a layby and said, "About here?"

He switched off the engine and they sat looking about them. "There's a deep ditch down there," said Agatha, looking to her left. "He wouldn't want to drag a body into the woods over there because he might be seen from the road. My guess is that he'd simply have rolled her down the bank."

"Let's search."

"In these heels?"

"I got Mrs. Freedman to give me the flat pair you keep in the office. They're in the bag I brought back with me. I brought a flask of coffee and some sandwiches."

For the first time, Agatha really warmed to him as she slipped off her high heels and put on her comfortable shoes. They left the car and slid down the bank and began searching among the bushes at the bottom. They'd gone at least a mile away from the car when Agatha panted, "It's no good. This is mad."

"Let's sit down. I've got the coffee."

Restored by two cups of black coffee, a chicken sandwich and a cigarette, Agatha looked around. Behind her, up on the dual carriageway, the traffic whizzed past. Round about them, the ground was dotted with litter thrown from cars. She looked idly to left and right and then exclaimed, "Knickers!"

"Yes, it is very hot," said Phil amiably.

"No, I mean I think that's a pair of knickers over there."

She got to her feet and went a little way to her left and stooped down. A brief torn pair of lace knickers was hanging on the twig of a stunted bush. "Could be any-one's," she muttered. "Let's look around here."

"Here's a shoe!" said Phil. "What was she wearing when she disappeared?"

"Let me think. A pink cropped top with sequins, jeans and high-heeled black sandals. No coat because the night was warm, and one of those things called bumbags although women usually wear them round the front."

"This is a black sandal. Should we call the police?"

"No, let's look further. If she had her knickers torn off and if it's Jessica, the jeans must be here somewhere."

Phil nipped back up the grass bank.

"Where are you going?" shouted Agatha.

"Get a better look from the top."

Agatha continued to move slowly along the ditch, parting the bushes, impervious to thorns catching at her tights.

"Someone's dumped an old fridge there," called Phil.

Agatha moved forward. The fridge, a large one, was lying on its side. Taking out a handkerchief, she opened the door. "Nothing!" she called.

"Let's keep trying."

"Maybe the police have been all over here."

"They missed the shoe and the knickers."

Agatha suppressed a groan. Then she decided instead of searching away from where the shoe had been found and keeping to the ditch, she should go back to the shoe and move forwards, away from the dual carriageway where the ground rose up again towards a wooded area.

She entered the trees, glad to get out of the sun. She was suddenly tired. The whole thing was useless. What could she find that teams of searchers could not? She turned to go back and the sun shone into her eyes, momentarily blinding her. She tripped over something and fell headlong.

"Snakes and bastards," muttered Agatha, heaving herself up on one elbow and twisting round to see what had tripped her. She found herself looking into a pair of staring dead eyes and flung herself backwards.

Jessica Bradley, naked from the waist down, and half covered with branches which had been torn out of the ground and put over the body to conceal it, lay sprawled like a broken doll. Agatha knew it was Jessica from the pink sequinned crop top, which had a huge bloodstain over most of the front. The body had probably been completely concealed, but predators had been at work and most of a leg had been chewed off.

"Phil!" screamed Agatha. She tottered

right out of the woods and then sat down and put her head between her knees.

Phil came running to join her. "She's in there. It's horrible, horrible," babbled Agatha.

"I'll phone the police," he said. "I'll photograph everything while we wait. Where is she?"

"In there," said Agatha, pointing.

Phil went into the woods and then, to her amazement, she could hear the busy click-click of his camera.

He came out and said, "I'll phone the police now."

Agatha felt some courage seeping back. "I'll phone the press. Don't want the police taking credit for this."

Soon they heard the wail of sirens in the distance. Police arrived first, then detectives, Agatha's friend Bill Wong amongst them, and then a forensic team.

Agatha and Phil told their stories over and over again and then were told to follow a police car to Mircester Police Headquarters to make their statements.

Agatha was interviewed by Detective Inspector Wilkes and Bill Wong. "Now, let's go over it again," said Wilkes.

And Agatha did, over and over.

When she was finished, she said, "Now I'd like to ask you a few questions."

"Haven't got the time," said Wilkes. "Wong, see her out."

"I'll nip over to your place sometime when I can get away," whispered Bill as he led her out.

"Oh, Mrs. Raisin!" Wilkes's voice sounded behind them in the corridor.

"Yes?"

"No talking to the press."

"If they ask me questions, then I will answer them," said Agatha.

"Bet you've phoned them already," murmured Bill.

Agatha found Phil waiting for her in reception and they left the police station together and straight into a crowd of reporters and photographers and television crews.

"I promised we wouldn't say anything to the press," whispered Phil urgently.

"Bollocks to that," said Agatha. "I have a business to run."

She faced up to the press. "I'll make one statement and then I'm off. It was a shocking discovery."

She was just about to brag that the discovery had been because of her brilliant intuition when she became sharply aware of

Phil standing beside her. Mrs. Bloxby's mild face rose before her eyes.

"It was the idea of my new photographer and, er, detective," said Agatha. She told them about Phil's idea but then bragged about how it was her idea to search in the woods.

She finished by saying, "That's all, folks."

As they were pushing their way through the press to get to Phil's car, one reporter shouted, "How old are you, Mr. Witherspoon?"

"Seventy-six," said Phil cheerfully.

"Oh, get in the car and drive off," snarled Agatha.

She had dealt with the press for a long time and knew that the innocent Phil had just stolen her moment of glory. There would be headlines in the tabloids about Grandpa Sleuth. Geriatric Sherlock. Pah.

Sir Charles Fraith had gone back to his own home to collect a few more things. He let himself in with a set of keys Agatha had given him a few years ago. He shooed her cats out into the garden after dumping his bag in the hall. Then he went into the sitting room, fixed himself a drink and turned on the television news.

He raised his glass to take a first sip and then froze as the announcer said, "A seventy-six-year-old grandfather, Phil Witherspoon, has discovered the body of the missing teenager, Jessica Bradley." There was a shot of Agatha and Phil leaving police headquarters and then the scene moved to outside Phil's cottage in Carsely. He looked flustered. "Really, it was all Mrs. Raisin's doing. I just made a few suggestions."

"How long have you been employed by the detective agency?"

"Today was my first day. I did suggest we go back and follow her route home and when we got to the dual carriageway, I did suggest she might have got into a car instead of crossing the road. It was then Mrs. Raisin took over and with a marvellous piece of detective work guessed where the body might be."

Like Agatha, Charles knew that Phil would turn out to be the hero of the day in the morning papers. He was seventy-six and at his first day of work. Poor Agatha.

Charles heard the front door crash open and hurriedly switched off the television set.

Agatha came in and stood glowering at him. "Bad day at the office, dear?" asked Charles.

She marched over to the drinks trolley and helped herself to a large gin and tonic, lit a cigarette and then slumped down on the sofa next to him.

"I employ some geriatric out of the kindness of my heart," she raged. "I find a body that the police couldn't find and he gets all the credit. I met Miss Simms on the road and she stopped my car and told me she had seen all the television cameras up at Phil's cottage. Have any of them been here?"

"Don't know. I've just arrived. But I hear the rumble of approaching vehicles. Probably them."

Agatha darted to the mirror and, opening her handbag, took out a lipstick and compact and began to make quick repairs to her make-up.

The doorbell rang. "I'll put them straight," she muttered.

"Aggie, if you do Phil down and contradict his story, you'll look ungracious and mean."

"Mind your own business."

The doorbell rang.

But Agatha was a shrewd operator. Charles heard her praising Phil and saying how lucky she was to have him. "I am tired of ageism," he heard Agatha say. "People should be employed because of their brains and talents irrespective of age." She then went on to credit Phil with the idea of retracing Jessica's journey home and then carefully went on to explain how her own brilliance and intuition had been instrumental in finding the body.

When she had finished, she came back in and sat down again on the sofa beside Charles. "Look at it this way," said Charles, "and be fair. If it hadn't been for Phil's idea you wouldn't have found the body."

"Oh, I suppose so. I suppose that case is over. I was charging the parents a modest fee. They don't have much, so I'd better leave the rest to the police."

"What's happened to your wits? You volunteer to find out who killed their daughter for nothing. Good publicity. And down under that hard shell of yours, there must be a decent human being who wants to find out who murdered a young girl."

A picture of Jessica's dead body rose up in Agatha's mind. "Excuse me," she gasped. She darted up to the bathroom and was violently sick.

After she had bathed her face and reapplied her make-up, she went shakily back downstairs.

"You're right," she said. "Publicity or not, I'll do it."

"Good. Let's walk up to Phil's cottage. The fresh air will do you good."

On the road there, they met Patrick Mulligan, a retired detective who had left Agatha's employ to live with Miss Simms. Miss Simms had been the unmarried mother of Carsely, her scandalous affairs with various married men delighting and shocking the village. People were almost disappointed that she had settled down.

"Saw that business on the news," said Patrick. "Funny, I've been getting bored and I was going to ask you for my old job back."

"Well, you're a day too late," said Agatha. But she stopped short, thinking that all the publicity would surely bring in new cases and Patrick still had ties to the police and was efficient at getting information out of them. "Oh, you can start again tomorrow, Patrick. Come with us to Phil's and we'll have a council of war."

When Phil let them in, Agatha was glad she had re-employed Patrick. Phil was looking older and quite frail.

"It's the shock," he said weakly. "It hits

you afterwards. For years I ran my own photographic shop in Evesham, nice quiet existence, chatting to the customers, and then this."

"It'll pass," said Agatha. "I've just been sick myself. By the way, are you a grandfather?"

"Never got married."

"The papers'll ignore that. Patrick, Phil came up with the idea that Jessica might have stopped on the dual carriageway, waiting to cross because it's a steep climb up to the bridge. He suggests she might have got into a car driven by someone she knew. We'll all start from there.

"Phil had better come with me to Ancombe tomorrow because we've got another case, but if you, Patrick, could start asking about uncles or friends or boyfriends, anyone the poor girl might have had the bad luck to trust." She glanced at her watch. "We're still in time to make the morning editions. Charles, could you phone the Associated Press and whomever and say I'm going to solve the murder for nothing?"

"Have you got numbers?"

"Right here." Agatha opened her capacious handbag and took out a thick notebook. "All the press numbers are here."

Charles retreated to the garden with his mobile phone and Agatha's book of numbers.

"I heard some bits and pieces," said Patrick. "Nothing really to help you. In these cases, the police look very hard at the family and relatives first. Then they search around for boyfriends. No particular boyfriend."

"I bet there was someone."

"Did you find out who she went clubbing with?" asked Patrick. "Girls of that age won't want to go to a disco alone."

"Her friends Fairy Tennant and Trixie Sommers. I've talked to them. I thought they were a bit cagey, but their parents kept interrupting."

"Okay. I'll try them both again. Why are you going to Ancombe?"

"Some businessman thinks his wife is cheating on him. She's going to be at a sale of work in Ancombe tomorrow. I want to have a really good look at her."

Agatha went to the office late in the morning after buying all the newspapers. As she had expected, Phil was prominently featured, but there was a paragraph in each newspaper saying that she was determined to solve the case and would not be charging the parents a fee.

"More cases, Mrs. Raisin," said Mrs. Freedman. "A missing husband, a missing teenager and two more cats."

"Give me the stuff on the missing people. I could really do with an animal detective."

"You need someone young and energetic who wouldn't charge much."

"Sounds as if you've got someone in mind."

"There's my nephew, Harry Beam. He's taking his gap year before starting university. I'm sure he'd do it just for expenses."

"I'll give him a trial. Get him to come along tomorrow. Now, I'm off. When Patrick comes into the office, give him the file on the two new missing people. On second thoughts, I won't take the files with me."

"Do you want me to phone him?"

"No, he's out checking on Jessica's friends. He thought he would try them at their school. I saw them with their parents present and it was a washout. He'll call in sometime or another."

Agatha drove to Carsely and collected Charles.

"Where's Phil?" he asked.

"Meeting us there."

When they arrived at the church hall in

Ancombe, it was to find Phil surrounded by admiring women, all praising him. Agatha scowled horribly but went up to Mrs. Bloxby.

"Is she here?"

"Over in the corner, selling jam. They won't think it odd of Phil to take photographs. He always does. And he's now a local celebrity."

"And a bachelor," said Agatha sourly. "Look at all those widows clustered round him."

"It is so good of you to employ him, Agatha. He does need the money."

Mrs. Bloxby fixed Agatha with her clear gaze. Agatha shifted uneasily, thinking of Phil's low wage. She realized she would need to give him a raise, and fast, or Mrs. Bloxby would haunt her conscience.

At first, she wondered whether she should approach Mabel Smedley. Everyone knew she was a detective. But surely quiet Mabel would not suspect for a moment that her husband would hire a detective to check up on her. She approached the jam stall and smiled at Mabel. "I don't think we've actually ever met," said Agatha.

Charles came to join Agatha. "I'm Agatha Raisin and this is my friend, Sir Charles Fraith."

Mabel Smedley was wearing a dreadful print dress, no make-up and her hair scraped back, but she turned out to have a beautiful smile which she directed at Charles.

"Did you make all this jam yourself?" asked Charles.

"Yes, I can recommend the strawberry."

"Oh, I'll buy a couple of pots of that. What about you, Agatha?"

"Eh? Oh, can you recommend anything else?"

"I think the quince jelly is all right. Rather nice with game."

"I'll have one of those, then."

Charles claimed to have left his money behind, so after glaring at him, Agatha paid for the jam.

"Your feet must get tired standing here all day," said Charles.

"I'm just about due for a break. Mrs. Henderson takes over for me. I see her coming."

"Such a hot day," said Charles. "Perhaps you might like to join me for a drink? Agatha can't come. She's supposed to be helping."

Agatha opened her mouth and shut it again.

Mrs. Henderson, a plump, sweating

woman with a round red face, came hurrying up. "I'm so sorry, I've got to go to the school. Dwayne's been playing up again, though if you ask me, that teacher's got it in for him and so I'll tell her."

"It's all right," said Charles. "Mrs. Raisin will take over for a bit. Won't you, Agatha?"

"Oh, all right," mumbled Agatha ungraciously.

"You are so kind," said Mrs. Smedley. "The prices are on all the jars."

Agatha gloomily watched as Charles went off with Mabel. Charles had borrowed a twenty-pound note from her.

"Aren't we going to the refreshment room?" asked Mabel.

"I saw a nice-looking pub across the road," said Charles, steering her out of the hall.

"I don't drink at this time of day."

"They'll have soft drinks or coffee."

They crossed the road and entered the pub. Mabel ordered a tonic water and Charles got himself a whisky.

They sat down at a corner table. Charles smiled at Mabel. "Tell me about yourself."

"There's not much to tell," said Mabel. "The Ancombe Ladies' Society keeps me busy. I make cakes and jam. I fund-raise for the homeless of Mircester. I drive the old folks on outings."

"Are you married?"

"Yes, and a very lucky woman. Not many women these days are allowed to stay at home. The modern husband wants his wife to make money. What about you, Sir Charles?"

"Just Charles. Oh, I deal with the accounts for the home farm. Then there are the cricket matches and fetes and concerts. The village always thinks it has a right to use my house and grounds for everything. I do a lot of gardening," lied Charles, who was beginning to feel, under her steady gaze, that he sounded like a dilettante.

"I love gardening. Tell me all about it."

Fortunately, Charles had a garrulous Scottish gardener who was always lecturing him on flowers, vegetables, trees and mulches. So he talked about gardening while she listened with a little half-smile on her face, the kind of smile you see on classical statues.

And then she suddenly rose to her feet. "I must get back. Do stay and finish your drink."

She gathered up her handbag and headed for the door. Then she turned and said sweetly, "Do tell your friend Mrs. Raisin that I didn't enjoy the film either. Pity. Such good reviews."

Three

Agatha was horrified when Charles told her of Mabel's parting comment. "I should never have employed an amateur like Phil," she raged.

"That's not fair, Agatha. Amateur yourself! If it hadn't been for Phil, you'd never have found Jessica's body, and both of you were tailing her. Mrs. Bloxby's trying to get your attention."

Agatha was aware of Mabel, back once more behind her jams, smiling that little smile.

"Oh, Mrs. Raisin, bad news," said Mrs. Bloxby. "Mabel has just confided in me that she knows you were following her. She thinks it's rather sweet."

"Sweet!"

"Yes, she says her husband is so jealous and it's very flattering."

"How did she know? We were well behind her."

"Perhaps she took out her compact or something to powder her nose in the cinema and spotted you."

"She doesn't wear make-up. Now what do I do?"

"Haven't you anyone else you could put on the case?"

"I've re-employed Patrick Mulligan. She doesn't know him. He's working on the Jessica Bradley case. We could switch."

"So you've re-employed Patrick. I thought you were cutting back on expenses."

"I'd forgotten the golden rule of business and that's to put money in to get money out. It looks, however, as if Mabel Smedley is a lot sharper than we thought."

Charles's mobile rang. He muttered an excuse and hurried outside.

Phil came up and Agatha told him about Mabel spotting them. "I don't know how she did it," he said. "I mean, she's not the suspicious type and all the ladies here think she's a perfect paragon. Works so hard for good causes . . ."

"And never was heard a discouraging word," said Agatha. "Let's get back to the office, Phil. We'd better put Patrick on it."

"But what about photographs?"

"We'll go on to the Jessica case. If Patrick digs up anything worth photographing, he can let us know."

Charles came back. "I've got to go," he said. "Remember my date who didn't show up? She's phoned to apologize. Her dog died and she was too distraught to get in touch with me."

"I'll drop you back at the cottage," said Agatha, "and you can collect your car."

She felt like snapping at Charles on the road back to Carsely. It was not as if she were jealous of this girl, she told herself. It was just annoying the way he dropped in and out of her life, using her cottage as a sort of hotel.

After Charles had collected his bags and left, Agatha felt the old wave of loneliness descend on her. Then she remembered Roy would be coming at the weekend and set out for the office feeling slightly more cheerful.

Before she left her cottage, she had phoned Patrick about the new arrangement. He was waiting for her when she arrived and listened intently as she outlined the case.

"Nobody's that perfect," he said. "I think she found out that her husband had employed you. I think I know how she found out." His eyes slid to where Mrs. Freedman was tapping away at the keys on the computer.

Agatha stared in amazement. "Mrs. Freedman. Stop work for a moment. Did you tell anyone that Robert Smedley had hired us to spy in his wife?"

Mrs. Freedman was a plump, placid lady with tightly curled grey hair, a pleasant face and thick glasses. A tide of red went up from her neck and covered her face.

"Do you remember the Boggles?"

"Can I ever forget them?" said Agatha. The Boggles were an elderly couple who had lived in Carsely and had demanded outings and treats from the members of the ladies' society with ruthless energy. Agatha had heaved a sigh of relief when they had relocated to a nursing home in Broadway.

"Paid them a little visit and they were asking about things. I didn't think there would be any harm in telling them."

"Harm?" raged Agatha. "They'd be on the phone as soon as you had left. You must never discuss anything that goes on here with anyone."

"Oh, I am so sorry. They looked so old and frail. I never believed for a moment they would phone anyone or tell anyone. I mean, they said that no one ever visited them."

"That's that," said Patrick. "She's not

going to do anything now that she knows we're on to her. Better tell Smedley."

"No, not yet," said Agatha slowly. "If there's anything to find out about her, it happened before, and that's what you've got to dig up."

"Do you want me to leave?" asked Mrs. Freedman in a quavering voice.

"Oh, go on with what you're doing," said Agatha.

The door opened and a young man slouched in. He had a shaven head, a nose stud, earrings and was dressed all in black — black T-shirt under a black leather jacket and black leather trousers. His face was set in a truculent sneer. He had blue eyes, a sharp nose and a long mouth.

"Hi," he said and slumped down on the sofa.

"My nephew, Harry Beam," said Mrs. Freedman.

For a moment, Agatha was lost for words. She had imagined the nephew would turn out to be a bright, clean-cut young man.

"So this is your gap year?" Agatha finally demanded.

"Yup."

"What are you going to study?"

"Physics."

"Where?"

"Imperial College."

How on earth did he get in there? wondered Agatha. Threaten to break their legs? Oh, well, one day should be enough to get rid of him.

"Mrs. Freedman, give Harry the files on the lost animals and let him get on with it. Patrick, did you manage to interview either Fairy Tennant or Trixie Sommers?"

"Not yet. I've been trying the neighbours. I was going to get them after school."

"Okay, Phil and I will go now."

"I know them," said Harry, looking up. "Pair of slags."

"How do you know them?"

"Year below me in school."

"And what about Jessica Bradley?"

"Naw, she was one of the quiet ones."

Agatha hesitated. The sensible thing would be to take Harry with her. But she balked at the thought of losing face by being seen with such an oaf.

"Come along, Phil. Harry, if you find one animal, you're hired."

He grunted, staring at the photographs of the missing pets.

Agatha sighed and went out, followed by Phil.

When they were driving off, she said, "I

begin to wonder about Mrs. Freedman. First she gossips and then she saddles me with that monster of a nephew."

"He may be all right," said Phil. "They all look weird these days."

They drove to Mircester High School and parked outside. Some parents were already waiting in their cars because a lot of pupils came in from outlying villages, some not served by a school bus.

At four o'clock, the pupils began to stream out. Agatha reflected that most seemed to have done everything they could to alter their school uniforms. A lot of the girls were wearing high heels and tiny skirts. The boys went in for the sloppy look. Trousers drooping over their ankles and shirt tails hanging out.

Agatha recognized Trixie and Fairy and walked towards them.

Harry Beam turned into a store where he knew there was a machine for printing business cards. He typed in his name, put "private detective" under it, the name of the agency and the phone numbers and email of the agency.

Then he got into an old white Ford van he had hired and headed out to the outskirts, where the Animal Rescue Shelter was located. It had just started up a month before.

He went into the reception desk.

The receptionist looked him up and down and demanded, "What do *you* want?"

And Harry smiled at her. The smile transformed him and Agatha would not have recognized his voice as he presented his business card and said meekly, "I wonder if I could look at your cats and dogs. You see, the owners are so distressed and we would like to do everything we can to help them find their pets."

She studied his card. "That's the agency which is helping poor Jessica's parents find out who murdered her?"

"That's the one."

"Wait here."

She went off.

Harry waited patiently. After a short time she returned with a man whom she introduced as Mr. Blenkinsop.

Mr. Blenkinsop had phoned the agency to check that Harry really was who he said he was.

"Follow me, young man," he said. "We'll let you have a look."

Clutching his folders, Harry followed him.

He went carefully from cage to cage, turning occasionally to ask when either a cat or dog had been admitted.

At last he said cheerfully, "I think I've got them all. Would you like to check the photographs with me as I point them out?"

Fairy and Trixie had the shortest skirts of all. They had both loosened their ties and unbuttoned their shirts to where an edge of brassiere would peep through. Both had very long legs ending in high heels. The school would have stopped short at allowing them to wear stilettos, so they had compromised by wearing black shoes with a heavy sole and large clumpy heel. They both had masses of brown unruly hair streaked blonde.

"Jail bait," muttered Phil. "How can their parents let them go around like that?"

Agatha walked forward. "Fairy and Trixie? Remember me?"

"That's us," said Fairy. "Who wants to know? Don't 'member you."

"I am a private detective investigating the death of Jessica Bradley."

"Look," said Trixie, "we've talked to the police. We don't need to talk to you. You don't look like a detective anyway. You're old."

"Cut the crap," said Agatha savagely. "I find it damned suspicious that you have no interest in finding out who murdered your friend."

They stared at her mulishly. Both were chewing gum. Then Trixie shrugged and said to Fairy, "Let's split."

They sauntered off, leaving Agatha glaring after them.

"I got their photos. Might come in useful," said Phil.

"Let's try the school," said Agatha. "So much bureaucracy and paperwork these days, the teachers are probably all still chained to their desks."

"I took notes from reports in the local papers. Her English teacher is a Miss Rook."

They entered the school and walked along corridors until they found a teacher who told them Miss Rook was in the staffroom and directed them there.

There were five teachers in the staffroom. "Miss Rook?" asked Agatha.

"That's me." A small woman got to her feet.

Agatha introduced herself and Phil.

"Is it about Jessica?"

"Yes."

"We'll leave you to it, Alice," said one of

the four other teachers, and then they left.

"Sit down," said Alice Rook. "Would you like some staff coffee? I warn you, it's pretty terrible."

"No, we're all right. Tell us about Jessica."

"Up till six months ago, she was a very good pupil. Not like some of the others, who shout Paki at me even though I'm half Indian."

"That explains the English name."

"Yes."

Alice Rook was a pretty woman with a smooth coffee-coloured skin, large dark eyes and thick black hair.

"So what caused the change in Jessica?"

"Fairy Tennant and Trixie Sommers. Bad influence. Jessica was quite shy, you know, and like all shy girls she wanted to be popular with the boys. She started to hang out with that precious pair. I told her her work was slipping, and that if she didn't get good grades she'd never make it to university. She just stared at me and said nothing. You know what I think? I think she had a crush on someone. I think she had decided to do anything to attract that someone."

"Any idea who that someone was?"

She shook her head. "I would swear it

was no one in her class or in her year. I know the boys the girls fancy and it wasn't any of them. I think it was someone outside of this school."

"What makes you say that?"

"I teach English, and for Jessica's form it's the last lesson of the day. Towards the end of the lesson, she would keep looking out of the window and fidgeting. Her eyes were bright and shining. She looked like a girl waiting for a lover."

"Did you ever see her go off with anyone?"

"I'm afraid not. What a waste of a bright girl."

"Is there a school counsellor? Might she have consulted someone?"

"There is a counsellor, Mrs. Aynton, but if Jessica consulted her, she can't really tell you anything. What the pupils say to her is confidential."

"But Jessica's dead! Surely that makes a difference."

"Wait here and I'll see if she's still in the building."

I went to a school like this, thought Agatha. Built of breeze block and already crumbling at the edges. Thrown up cheap. The smells are the same. Disinfectant and the metallic odour of school meals.

Alice Rook came back. She shook her head. "Jessica never consulted the school counsellor."

"What was her best subject?" asked Phil.

"Definitely maths. The only subject she still got A's in."

"Who taught her?"

"Mr. Owen Trump. Why?"

"Pupils will always work hard for a teacher they admire and she might have said something to him," said Phil. "Is he still in the school?"

"I'll have a look."

Agatha was torn between wishing she had thought of that idea herself and a feeling that she really ought to give Phil a little praise. Instead, she said, "We'll review your wages when we get back to the office. I think we can say your trial is over."

Phil's face lit up. "Thank you very much."

"Only what you deserve," said Agatha gruffly.

The staffroom door opened and a young man came in. "I'm Owen Trump," he said. "Alice has gone home."

Agatha's heart gave a lurch. He looked in the dim room like a younger version of James Lacey. He had thick black hair and bright blue eyes. "I'll put the light on," he said. "I think we're going to get rain at last."

He switched on the light and Agatha realized he wasn't like James Lacey at all. His face was handsome but not as strong and he was wearing blue contact lenses. Where as James Lacey's mouth was long and firm, his was full-lipped and sensuous.

"How can I help you?" he asked. He sat down in a battered armchair by the two-bar electric fire, and Agatha and Phil, who had risen when he entered, resumed their seats.

"As Miss Rook probably told you," began Agatha, "I am a private detective investigating the death of Jessica Bradley."

"That was an awful business. She was my brightest pupil."

"She had fallen off in all her other subjects," said Agatha. "Did she have a crush on you?"

"Oh, well," he said with an irritating air of complacency, "they all have a crush on me from time to time."

"So did she confide in you?"

"No. She would sometimes stay behind to ask me some question about maths."

"Did you ever see her outside school?"

"What exactly are you implying?"

Agatha back-pedalled. "I mean, did you

ever see her in Mircester after school hours with anyone?"

"Only with that precious pair, Fairy and Trixie, in the mall. I hardly recognized Jessica. They were all in school uniform, but Jessica had hitched up her skirt and she was heavily made up."

"What were they doing?"

"They were waiting under the clock in the centre of the mall. It's a favourite meeting place. I assumed they were waiting for boys."

"Did Jessica show any interest in any boy in the school?"

"Not that I know of. You see, she was always a quiet, scholarly girl, up until about six months ago. I didn't notice much difference, but her other teachers wondered what had happened to her. If that is all . . . ?"

Agatha gave him her card. "If you hear anything that might be important, let me know."

"I will let the police know. They are better equipped to deal with this." And with that, he walked out.

"Pompous twit," muttered Agatha. "And vain. Did you notice those contact lenses?"

"No, but a lot of people wear them. How can you tell?"

"It's that unnatural bright blue. Well, I

suppose we'd better get over to the mall. I've got a photograph of Jessica. We'll see if any of the shopkeepers near the clock recognize her, although this photograph makes her look just like a decent schoolgirl, and if she was heavily made-up, they might not remember her. Still, it's worth a try."

But the shopkeepers could not remember seeing Jessica. "I took photos of Fairy and Trixie," said Phil. "I'll get them printed up and try again tomorrow if you like. If they recognize Fairy and Trixie, they might remember a third girl. What now?"

"We'll go back to the office and start again tomorrow. I need to get rid of Harry Beam."

Harry Beam was slouched on the sofa. On the floor in front of him were three cat boxes and a small Jack Russell was sitting on his lap.

"Good heavens!" said Agatha. "You've found them all. How did you do it?"

Harry had told Mrs. Freedman not to say he had found them all at the animal refuge. "Just walking miles looking and looking."

Agatha regarded him suspiciously. "Are

you sure you've got the right animals? Let me see the photos."

She studied the photos and the animals.

"Am I hired?" asked Harry.

"I suppose so," said Agatha ungraciously. Then an idea struck her. "Do you feel like working tonight?"

"Sure. What is it? More cats?"

"No. I would like you to go to that disco Jessica visited on the night she was murdered. You look the part. Get friendly with the young people and see what you can find out. Have you phoned the owners of the cats and that dog?"

"Thought you might like to do that personally and phone the local rag so they can photograph the happy reunion."

"Right." Agatha arranged a wage for Harry and an increased wage for Phil with Mrs. Freedman and then phoned the owner of the animals, telling them all to call at the office at six o'clock and then phoned the local paper.

After she had dealt with the delighted owners and posed with them for photographs, Patrick arrived.

"Anything?" asked Agatha.

"I went to the village pub for starters. Smedley is disliked, but everyone thinks his wife is a saint. There's a rumour he beats her. His electronics factory is out on the industrial estate. They have a show-room, so I went out there and pottered around. I talked to the sales staff, asked them about their boss and all that. Don't like him. Asked if they'd ever met the wife and they brightened up. Say she's a gem. He's so mean that he gets his wife to do all the catering for the Christmas party. They said the food was great and she was abso-lutely charming. Brick wall so far. But I'll keep at it."

Phil said, "Maybe if Harry comes home with me, I can print up the photos of Trixie and Fairy and let him see them. If they're at the club tonight, maybe he can get into conversation with them."

"He knows them. Remember? But print them up anyway."

Agatha was just microwaving her dinner that evening when the doorbell rang. She found Bill Wong on the step. "I couldn't get round earlier," he said.

"Come in," said Agatha. "I was just about to have dinner. Want some?"

"No, I've had something in the canteen. What have you been up to?"

Agatha told him about Owen Trump. "Clever work," said Bill. "I never thought of a schoolteacher."

Agatha felt a little guilty twinge. It had been Phil's idea.

"What about your end?" she asked. "Her English teacher thinks Jessica may have been in love. English was last period and she said Jessica kept looking out of the window."

"That doesn't sound like one of the schoolboys."

"She also said her work had deteriorated in the last six months, apart from maths."

"We'll have a look at this maths teacher. So how are you? Heard from James Lacey?"

"No," said Agatha curtly.

"No new interesting neighbours?"

"The house is up for sale again. Probably be the middle-aged or elderly who'll buy it. Young people can't afford the prices around here."

"So how's the agency doing?"

"Work's picking up. I took on a divorce case. I don't think it's really a divorce case. I think it's a neurotic husband who is insanely jealous. His wife is regarded as a saint."

"There are no saints, Agatha."

"There's Mrs. Bloxby."

"Come on. She's only human like the

rest of us. Oh, listen. There's the rain at last."

Agatha surveyed him fondly. Bill, half Chinese and half English, had been her first friend. He was of medium height with black hair and brown almond-shaped eyes.

"Would you like a drink?"

"No, thank you," said Bill, unwinding Hodge from his neck. "I've got to go. Why don't you come for dinner with us one night?"

Agatha repressed a shudder. Much as she loved Bill, she found his parents terrifying. Besides, his mother was a rotten cook and even a lifetime of microwaved meals could not inure Agatha to the overcooked meat and soggy vegetables that made up Mrs. Wong's favourite cuisine.

"I'd like that," she lied. "Wait until things have slacked off a bit."

When Bill had left, she opened the kitchen door and stood under the shelter of the overhanging thatch. She had recently employed a woman gardener and the long strip of garden was a blaze of flowers. She did wish Bill had not mentioned James Lacey. She often passed days at a time now without thinking about him or wondering if he ever thought of her.

Loneliness gripped her again and as she turned to go indoors, she felt that irritating stabbing pain in her hip. After Roy's visit, she would make an appointment with Richard Rasdall, the masseur in Stow. All she needed was a bit of limbering up.

Four

Harry Beam entered the disco and looked around.

He had visited it before, but only on Saturday nights, and he was surprised to find it so full on a weekday.

He wondered if the police ever raided the place because there were underage youths and girls drinking Bacardi Breezers at the bar while crowds of them gyrated to deafening music under the strobe lights.

He made his way to the bar and ordered a beer. Then he turned and leaned his back on the bar and studied the dance floor. And then he saw them. They were heavily made up.

Harry finished his beer. Trixie was dancing with Fairy. "Mind if I cut in?" He looked at Trixie. Fairy shrugged and headed off to the bar. Trixie threw herself all over the place, seemingly unaware of his presence. Harry realized it would be impossible to talk to her in the disco because of the noise level. He would need to court her for a boring length of time and then offer to take her home. So he danced with her and bought her drinks and at last she glanced at her watch and said, "Gotta go."

"I'll take you home," shouted Harry.

"Got a car?"

"I've got my motorbike tonight."

"Cool."

Outside, he gave her his spare helmet. "Where to?" asked Harry. Trixie gave him her home address. He registered that it was two doors away from where Jessica lived. He was just wondering how to manufacture a stop somewhere so that he could talk to her when she said, "Can we go round to where Jessica's body was found?"

"Sure," said Harry. She climbed on the back and they roared off.

Harry knew as he sped along the dual carriageway that he would recognize the spot from the police tape. He just hoped there wouldn't be any police on duty because they would quickly move them on.

He slowed and stopped when he saw the police tape. The earlier rain of the evening had stopped and a dank mist was swirling around the scene.

He parked the bike and he and Trixie got off. She removed her helmet and her eyes gleamed with excitement in the dark.

"Let's do it here," she said. "Down in the grass."

"And get my leathers mucky," said Harry.

"You a poofter or something?"

"Listen, babes. The forensics will be back in the morning and I don't want my DNA spread over the grass. You're weird."

She stared at him sulkily. "Don't you fancy me?"

"I did but right now I don't," said Harry. "What was a nice girl like Jessica Bradley doing having a friend like you?"

"She wasn't no angel. I could tell you a thing or two."

"Go on. Bet you know nothing."

"I tell you, she was having it off with a man old enough to be her father."

"Who?"

"Kiss and tell."

Harry repressed a sigh and clamped his mouth over hers. Her tongue went so far down his throat he was frightened he would gag.

When he finally came up for air, he asked again, "Who?"

"Salesman at that electronics factory. Smedleys Electronics. Name's Burt Haviland."

"I'd never have believed it," said Harry. "Now let's get you home."

Agatha was awakened at midnight by a call from Harry. He told her about Burt Haviland.

"Good work," said Agatha.

"Do you want me to come with you when you interview him?"

"I'll need to think about it. I'm awfully afraid we might have to tell the police."

"Why?"

"If we go to the factory, we might run into Smedley, who'd get huffy if he thought we weren't solely on his case. Then this Burt can simply give us a flat denial. The police can take his DNA and compare it to anything they might have found at the autopsy. I'll ask Patrick and see you first thing at the office."

Agatha rang Patrick. The former Miss Simms answered the phone. "Wot you doing ringing in the middle of the night, Mrs. Raisin?" she demanded.

"I want to speak to Patrick."

"I wish you'd left him alone. He's never here and I've got to look after the kids meself. What fun's that? I think he's too old for me. I mean, old is all right in gentlemen friends, if you get my meaning. Besides, he's only got his pension and I've had to take a part-time at the supermarket."

"I never thought you were mercenary," said Agatha, momentarily diverted.

"Like them men who go out to wars?"

"No, after money."

"Who isn't these days? It's all right for you. I'll get him."

Agatha heard her say, "Wake up. It's Mrs. Raisin on the line."

"What does she want?" grumbled Patrick.

"Ask her and find out. I'm going back to sleep."

When Patrick came on the line, Agatha told him what Harry had found out, ending with, "Should I tell the police?"

"I think you'd better."

"Any results from the autopsy? Was she raped?"

"Too early to say."

"I'll phone Bill Wong."

Agatha found Bill's mobile phone number, praying the phone would be switched on, otherwise she would have to call his home number and maybe get one of his frightening parents.

To her relief, Bill answered his mobile. She told him what Harry had found out.

"Oh, good work," said Bill. "We'll pull him in first thing tomorrow."

"You owe me," said Agatha. "I want you

to come round here when you can and let me know the result."

After two busy following days — two divorce cases had come in and three missing pets — Agatha was glad to see Roy getting off the evening train at Moreton-in-Marsh. His thin hair was jelled up into spikes on his head, revealing, as he bent over the boot to put his travel bag in, that he had a tattoo of entwined snakes on his neck.

"Handling a pop group?" asked Agatha.

"Yes, the Busy Snakes. They're hot and they think I'm cool."

"Roy, you're like a chameleon. You change according to whoever you're doing public relations for. I never bothered."

"I'm not as pushy as you, sweetie."

"But a tattoo? Have you considered the agony of getting that removed once tattoos become unfashionable?"

"Don't tell anyone. It's a transfer."

"I was hoping to discuss a couple of cases with you but how can you go detecting with me when you look like that?"

Roy got into the passenger seat. "Don't nag. I'll wash my hair and scrub off the fake tattoo. I hope we're eating out."

"No."

"Aggie, much as I love you, I haven't got

your palate for microwaved meals."

"It's all right. It's a carry-out from a very good Chinese place in Stow."

As they ate that evening, Agatha told him about the Smedleys and then about finding Jessica's body.

"That's amazing," said Roy. "Imagine you finding her when the police couldn't."

Agatha's conscience gave a twinge. "Well, it was Phil's idea, really."

"Who's Phil?"

"He's a seventy-six-year-old photographer who lives in the village."

"There you are. Age does bring wisdom."

"Not really," said Agatha. "I've found that stupid young people grow up to be stupid old people."

"You haven't really softened up after all. Sometimes I wonder why you don't just chuck it all in and retire gracefully. I would."

"What! You? Out of all the trendy excitement of London!"

"You know what it's like. Public relations can be wearing. Being nice to some truly awful people. The Busy Snakes have one hit record and already they're all prima donnas. They were lucky, that's all. By next year, no one will have heard of them and they won't have any money for their drugs and they'll be out mugging old ladies for a fix."

"You *are* gloomy."

"I tell you, a month ago I was driving down one of the motorways. It was a windy day and I saw them erecting a circus tent in a field by the road. I had this sudden fantasy that the wind would blow the tent away, right across my car. I'd make an emergency stop. The circus people would come running and pull the canvas off my car and ask if I was all right. They'd invite me back for tea and I would join the circus and I would never see another pop star again."

There was a silence.

Then Agatha said, "I suppose you imagined the circus people in full costume."

"Of course. The horse riders had their scarlet coats and plumed hats and the trapeze artist, she was in sequins. She had long dark hair and it brushed across my face as I sat at the wheel when she leaned in the window."

"When did you last have a holiday, Roy?"

"Can't quite remember. I just begin to plan and something else turns up."

"When you go back," said Agatha bracingly, "book a holiday right away. Go somewhere where you can lie on the beach and think of nothing."

"Can't. The Busy Snakes are booked for Wembley."

"Didn't know they were that important."

"They aren't. They're warming up for Elton John."

"Well, after that . . ."

"Maybe. So are we detecting this weekend?"

"After having listened to you, I think we both need time off. I know, we'll motor to Bath on Sunday and have an enormous cream tea and then sit in the gardens and listen to the brass band."

"That sounds great. Give murder and mayhem a rest."

The following day was perfect weather with castles of white clouds piled up over a large blue sky.

Anaesthetized by the largest cream tea they had ever eaten — Roy had insisted on two lots of scones, strawberry jam and Cornish cream — they slumped down in deckchairs in the gardens and listened to the band, surrounded by the amiable chatter of families with their children.

Roy had bought a Panama hat and it was

now tilted across his eyes. Agatha did not have a hat but she had edged her deckchair under the shade of a tree.

After a few minutes, Roy let out a faint snore. Maybe he was right, thought Agatha. Maybe she should give up the whole business of detecting. But she knew all at once that if she spent too much time alone she would start thinking of James Lacey again. Still, at least she actually cared about poor Jessica and was determined to find out who murdered the girl. Robert Smedley was another matter. And then she blinked rapidly. At first she thought her mind had conjured up an image of him. Then she realized it really *was* Robert Smedley. He had risen from a deckchair near the bandstand and was helping a young woman to her feet. The woman was vaguely pretty in a vapid kind of way. Lots of red hair but a thin white face and a rabbity mouth.

"Roy!"

Snore.

Agatha leaned over and prodded him in the ribs.

"Hey, what?"

"It's Smedley," hissed Agatha, "with another woman."

"Where?"

"Over there. They're coming this way. Here!"

Agatha extracted a newspaper from the three she had been holding in her lap. Roy snatched one and opened it up to shield his face. Agatha did the same. They covertly lowered the newspapers a little.

Robert Smedley was dressed in white flannels and a tight blazer with a flashy crest on the pocket. His lady was wearing very high heels and leaning on his arm. They waited until the couple had passed.

"Right!" hissed Agatha. "We follow them."

But too many junk meals had taken their toll and Agatha's hips were wedged firmly into the deckchair. She stood up with the chair sticking to her backside. "Help me, Roy."

He wrenched her free. There was a ripple of laughter from the other people in deckchairs. Agatha looked wildly round. Smedley and his companion had disappeared.

"You need to lose weight," said Roy.

"I've only put on a little. It was that cream tea. They were heading up the hill."

They hurried up to Pierrepoint Street. "No sign," panted Agatha. "I'll go right and you got left."

"I don't know what they look like. They were gone by the time I looked!"

"He's portly with thinning hair, tight blazer, white trousers. She's rabbity with red hair, lots of it, wearing a blue-and-white-patterned dress and very high heels. She can't have got far in those heels. We'll meet back here."

They split up. Agatha went as far as the Grand Parade on her side and Roy went along Manvers Street, Dorchester Street and then St. James's Parade.

When they met up again, they were hot and tired. "I know," said Agatha. "Hotels."

"There are loads of hotels. Loads!" screeched Roy.

"Let me think. He was so solicitous, I think it must be a new love, so he'd take her somewhere posh."

"Like where?"

"Like the Granton Crescent Hotel. We'd better get a cab. It's a long climb up."

But there did not seem to be any cabs available. By the time they had trudged up to the Royal Crescent, where the hotel was situated, Roy was flushed with heat and cross with Agatha.

They entered the cool hallway of the hotel and approached the reception desk. "Yes, madam?"

The receptionist was cool, slim and foreign.

"I wonder if a friend of mine has checked in?" asked Agatha. "A Mr. Smedley?"

Long painted nails rattled efficiently over the keys of a computer. The receptionist raised her head. "I am afraid we have no one of that name."

"May I just see the book? Such a rogue. He may have signed in under another name."

"What book?"

"The book the guests sign," said Agatha impatiently.

"No, that is so old-fashioned. They sign cards and their bookings are logged on the computer."

"Oh, if you could just give me a printout."

"The details are private. Please leave." The receptionist turned away to where an overdressed woman was waiting. "Mrs. Bentinck, how nice to see you again."

Agatha saw a bar leading off the hall. "I'm having a nice cold drink."

"Remember, you're driving," cautioned Roy.

"I don't think one mimsy gin and tonic is going to make a blind bit of difference. Come on."

The bar was cool and dark. Agatha lowered herself into an armchair with a sigh of relief and wiggled her toes inside her sandals.

A waiter came up and they gave their orders. When they had been served, Roy said, "I know you like to take long shots, but this was a very long one indeed."

"I know," conceded Agatha. "Still, I must have lost some weight with all that walking. I'll tell Patrick about it." She took out her mobile phone. "He's supposed to be on the Smedley case and I'm supposed to be finding Jessica's murderer. Now I feel guilty for having taken time off."

She spoke to Patrick and then said, "We'll collect the car and park somewhere on the road out. See if we can catch them leaving. I mean, it's Sunday. Maybe he wants to get home before the wife suspects anything. Maybe he's not booked into a hotel."

"They may not be leaving," complained Roy as they sat in the sun inside the car by the side of a road leading out of Bath.

"This is the road they'll take if they're heading back to the Cotswolds."

"But they may be shacked up somewhere for another night of mad passion.

86

Isn't there any air conditioning in this car?"

"No."

"What happened to the Saab? What happened to the Audi? Why are we sitting in a small hatchback Rover which looks as if it had five hundred previous owners?"

"I wanted an anonymous-looking car. No one notices a cheap car. This is a very good Rover and I got it second-hand. Keep your eyes on the road behind."

"It's all right for you. You've got the rear-view mirror. I've got a crick in the neck from twisting around."

"Phil's got the number of the wife's car," said Agatha half to herself. "He wouldn't be driving that. I wonder if he knows the number of Smedley's car."

She phoned Phil and asked him. "Yes, I've got it," said Phil. "I went round after dark and photographed both cars in the driveway. It's a BMW. Dark green." He gave her the registration number.

Agatha thanked him, rang off, and gave Roy the details. They waited patiently. "This is hopeless . . ." Roy was beginning to say, when Agatha exclaimed, "Here they come!"

The BMW driven by Smedley roared past.

Agatha set off in pursuit.

"I don't think you should be so close behind him," shouted Roy over the noise of the engine. "Let another car get in between you and him."

But Agatha hung on grimly, only glad that Smedley showed no sign of exceeding the sixty-mile-an-hour speed limit.

Smedley cut off the A-4 and onto the A-365. "Where's he going?" muttered Agatha. On they flew in pursuit — the A-365, then the A-361, A-360, and turned off again on the A-344. "Is he going to Amesbury?" wondered Agatha.

"I think he's going to Stonehenge," said Roy.

Sure enough, that turned out to be where Smedley was headed. A car park attendant directed Smedley to a parking place on the right and then guided Agatha down to one on the far left.

"Quick!" said Agatha, turning off the engine. "We don't want to lose him now."

They scrambled out of the Rover and ran to where they had seen Smedley directed to park — just in time to see the BMW roaring out of the car park.

"I told you not to drive so close," grumbled Roy. "They must have seen us and driven in here to shake us off."

They went back to their car and Agatha set off in pursuit, but nowhere on the road back did they spot the BMW.

They drove to Ancombe. Roy, instructed by Agatha, got out and crept up the Smedleys' drive. He returned with the news that the BMW was parked outside. "He must have dropped her off somewhere or maybe it'll turn out she was a family relative and the wife knows he was taking her for an outing."

That evening Agatha drove Roy down to the station to catch the London train and then returned to find Bill Wong waiting for her.

"What's the news about Haviland?" asked Agatha eagerly.

"Let me inside and make me a coffee and I'll tell you."

Seated in the kitchen over mugs of coffee, Bill said, "Haviland was dating Jessica. He's in his thirties. They didn't want the parents to know, him being so much older. He's got a good alibi."

"Like what?"

"He's a sales rep for Smedleys Electronics. He was down in Exeter for a week and just got back when we picked him up. He was attending a convention at a hotel there. We checked it out and he never left Exeter."

"He could have done," said Agatha. "I mean, conventions are such boozy affairs, he could have nipped back and no one would have noticed. They can check his DNA —"

"That's the trouble. Jessica was not sexually assaulted."

"But she was naked from the waist down! And I found a pair of ripped knickers."

"Jessica Bradley was a virgin."

"What! In this day and age? Going to the club and dating an older man?"

"I tell you, this Burt Haviland was definitely in love with her. He's really cut up about everything."

"So did she tell him anything about anyone? Anyone she was frightened of?"

Bill shook his head. "Haviland said they were waiting until she finished school and then they were going to announce their engagement."

"I'd like a word with him. What's his address?"

"I'm not supposed to give you information like that, Agatha."

"You know I can find it. No one needs to know you told me."

"Oh, all right. He lives at number ten Bascombe Way in Mircester out on that council estate."

"All roads seem to lead to Smedleys Electronics," said Agatha. She told Bill about spotting Smedley with a woman in Bath and ended by saying, "Maybe all that stuff about his wife is guff. Maybe he wanted his wife to find out to throw her off the scent."

"If Smedley spotted you following him, he'll be in the office tomorrow to cancel your investigation."

Not only Robert Smedley turned up in Agatha's office the following morning but his wife, Mabel, as well.

Five

They came in, holding hands, and beaming all around. Agatha wished in that moment that Harry Beam was out. The young man was slumped on the sofa with a can of Diet Coke in his hand. He was wearing a denim jacket and jeans torn at the knees.

"I have happy news," said Smedley. "I no longer need your services. It was all a mistake. I am afraid I am so in love with Mabel that I am inclined to be stupidly jealous."

As if he saw, hovering on Agatha's lips, the question, "What were you doing in Bath with a young lady?" he added quickly, "Of course, I wouldn't dream of asking you for a refund and please bill me for any expenses."

"Thank you," said Agatha, wondering whether to bill him for expenses for a trip to Bath and then rejecting the idea. He had already paid a great deal of money. She was supposed to have been spying on Mrs. Smedley, not Mr. Then she wondered why he was not asking for any of his money back.

"I am very pleased that things have worked out for you, Mr. and Mrs. Smedley. May I offer you some coffee?"

"No, we must be off," he said jovially.

Harry Beam appeared to rouse himself from some sort of torpor. "That's a nasty bruise you've got on your arm, Mrs. Smedley."

She was carrying a light jacket and immediately put it on. For one moment, something unpleasant flicked at the back of Smedley's eyes as he surveyed Harry.

"And who are you, might I ask?"

"Harry Beam, detective. I'm on undercover work."

"From your appearance, it must be something really unsavoury. Come, Mabel."

When they had left, Agatha asked, "Was there really a bruise? I wasn't looking."

"A whopping great one, as if someone had grabbed her arm and twisted it."

"If he's hurting her, she should go to the police." Patrick came in and Agatha told him the Smedley case was over. He was followed by Phil, who said he had good photos of Trixie and Fairy.

"Right, Phil," said Agatha. "We'll get

down to the mall. Patrick, the latest is that Jessica was not raped but it was made to look that way. This boyfriend appears to have a clear alibi, but go and see if you can talk to him. He might have something interesting to say about Jessica that he's forgotten."

"This murder looks like the work of an amateur," said Patrick. "These days most people would know that with DNA they'd soon find out she hadn't been raped."

"Maybe not. They might assume the police would think a condom had been used. Whoever did it didn't know she was a virgin."

"What about me?" asked Harry.

"There are two outstanding divorce cases, both well-to-do people, so you'll need to blend in. Different clothes and no studs."

She expected him to protest, but he gave a laconic "Okay."

"Mrs. Freedman will give you the files."

"You've got the photographer," said Harry. "You want me to take a camera?"

Agatha was reluctant to surrender Phil. He was proving to have a good insight into things.

"Come down to my car," said Phil, "and

I'll fix you up with a proper camera and a telescopic lens."

"Cool."

"What should I be working on?" asked Patrick.

"See if you can have a chat with Burt Haviland."

Agatha and Phil set out for the mall. The recent rain had left the skies grey and the air muggy and stifling.

They went back to the clock and, armed with the pictures of Trixie, Fairy and Jessica, began to quiz the shopkeepers round about, but although four of them recognized the girls, it was always the same story. They had seen them waiting but after that had not noticed anything else.

"I think it's time we went back and saw the parents," said Agatha. "The body won't have been released for burial yet, so they'll probably just be sitting around. I'd like to ask them about Burt Haviland. That sounds like a name out of a romance. Be interesting to find out if he changed his name at any time."

Mrs. Bradley opened the door to them, looking like a zombie. Agatha guessed she had probably been prescribed tranquillizers.

"Oh, Mrs. Raisin. So kind of you to still offer to find Jessica's murderer. Do come in."

Her voice had a soft Gloucestershire burr.

They went into a pleasant living room. There was a large photograph of Jessica on the sideboard, looking every inch the correct English schoolgirl.

Pretty net curtains fluttered at the open windows and the room was full of domestic clutter: books and magazines, videos, and a discarded piece of knitting.

"Is your husband home?" asked Agatha.

"He's gone back to work at the ice cream factory. He says it keeps his mind off the horror of it all."

"You should try one of those bereavement counselling classes," said Agatha gently. "Tranquillizers only keep the grief damped down and it can erupt worse later on. I'll find out where the nearest one is for you."

"Thank you." Tears spilled down her cheeks, rolling down silently, one after the other.

"I'll make tea," said Phil.

Mrs. Bradley mopped her eyes with a tissue.

"Did you know Jessica had a boyfriend?"

She looked at Agatha in amazement. "No, was it one of the boys at school?"

"It was a man of thirty-five called Burt Haviland. Works in sales at Smedleys Electronics."

"She said nothing of this to us."

"It appears Jessica may have been frightened you'd stop him seeing her because he was so much older. He appears to have been very much in love with her. He has an alibi. Mrs. Bradley, your daughter was not raped. The police will no doubt inform you. Jessica was a virgin."

"My poor little girl." She began to cry again.

Agatha suddenly wished she was the type of woman who would find it easy to cross the room and give Mrs. Bradley a comforting hug, but she wasn't, so she made what she hoped were sympathetic noises.

Phil came in with the tea things. "I've made yours very sweet," he said to Mrs. Bradley. "Good for shock."

She gave him a weak smile and sipped her tea.

Seeing she was once more composed, Agatha asked, "May we see Jessica's room?"

"Please go upstairs. It's at the top on the left. I won't go up with you. I can't."

Agatha and Phil went up the stairs and pushed open the door of Jessica's room. They each pulled on a pair of latex gloves. It looked the usual teenager's room with posters of pop stars on the walls, but with more books than usual. There was a computer desk against the wall but no computer. Agatha guessed the police must have taken it away to find out if she had been communicating with anyone on the Internet.

She pulled open the drawer on the desk. "I suppose if she had a diary, the police will have that as well. Unless she hid it. Where would a teenager hide a diary?"

"Don't know," said Phil. "Let's search."

They began to search everywhere in the room. There was a chest of drawers. Agatha pulled out each drawer and felt underneath. Nothing.

"Let's try the desk." There were three drawers. Agatha began to slide them out one by one. The bottom drawer stuck a little and Agatha gave it an impatient wrench. It clattered onto the floor and a packet of letters which had been taped to the underside of the drawer spilled across the floor.

They gathered up the letters. They were all addressed to Jessica, care of Sommers.

"That's Trixie and her address," said Agatha. "She must have been using Trixie to get letters from her boyfriend." She gently spread out the envelopes on the desk.

"We'll split them up. There are twelve here. You take six and I'll take the other."

They turned out to be passionate love letters from Burt. It was evident he hoped to marry her as soon as she had finished school.

"There's something here," said Phil. "He says in this letter that he's worried that Jessica was letting her friends blackmail her into going clubbing with them. 'If Trixie and Fairy are threatening to tell your teachers, then let them. I don't like you going around with that precious pair. The other thing with them is just a laugh, just work.' "

"That's interesting. What other thing? It's time we had a talk with those girls after school."

"What do we do with the letters? Hand them over to the police?"

"No, there's nothing there that can really help them."

"Yes, there is," said Phil. "It sheds a new light on why she was seen with Trixie and Fairy. And I wonder as well about that 'other thing' she refers to."

"Let's leave poor Jessica a bit of privacy. We'll put them back. I mean, it's awfully romantic to send letters in this day and age instead of texting and emailing."

They went downstairs and Agatha asked Mrs. Bradley, "Weren't you worried about Jessica going out clubbing?"

"Yes, I was. But she had changed. She said all the girls did it. She was always home on time until the last night."

"Did the police take away her computer?"

"They wanted to check if she'd been in contact with anyone on the Internet, but I told them my husband was always afraid of girls getting into one of those chat rooms and meeting a pervert and he used to check all her emails."

The Bradleys were turning out to be stricter than Agatha had imagined. "Did Jessica have a mobile phone?"

"Frank, that's my husband, wouldn't let her have one. She begged for one, but he said that perverts were texting schoolgirls. I suppose that's why we let her go clubbing, but just the once a week. We didn't want to put too many restrictions on her and they do grow up so fast these days."

They promised to let Mrs. Bradley know

as soon as they found anything and left.

"Why," asked Agatha as she got into the passenger seat of Phil's old Ford, "would Trixie and Fairy blackmail her into going out with them?"

"Jealousy," said Phil. "Good scholar. Probably wanted to make her as low as they are."

"I'm starving," said Agatha. "Let's have something to eat."

Agatha's mobile phone rang just as they were finishing lunch. It was Bill Wong. "Where are you?" he asked.

"Just left Mrs. Bradley's house. Why?"

"The Smedleys came to see you this morning, didn't they?"

"Yes, both of them. Very lovey-dovey. Smedley asked me to drop the case. Why?"

"Smedley's just been found dead in his office. We think it's poisoning. You'd better come here to police headquarters and make a statement."

Agatha and Phil were interviewed by Bill Wong and Detective Chief Inspector Wilkes.

Agatha told them about the visit of the Smedleys. Then she remembered about Harry noticing a bruise on Mrs. Smedley's arm. "He could have been beating her. Oh, there's something else." She told them about being with Roy in Bath and seeing Smedley with a young woman.

"Description?" snapped Wilkes.

"Lots of red hair, sort of pretty but with a pale face and a rabbity mouth. Good figure."

"We'll look into it. Could be one of his employees. Sounds like his secretary. All right. From the beginning. They came into your office this morning . . ."

"Didn't you get it the first time?" demanded Agatha crossly. But Bill Wong flashed her a warning look so she went over the whole thing again.

Finally they were told they were free to go. "She must have cracked and poisoned him," said Agatha outside police headquarters.

"They'll have a hard time proving that if she wasn't at the office with him," said Phil. "Maybe it was that rabbity girl. Anyway, it's police business now."

They went back to the office. Patrick Mullen phoned. "I tracked down Burt at a shop in Oxford. We went for a coffee. I swear the man's sincere and in a miserable state of grief."

"Two things, Patrick. Can you catch him again and ask him about a red-haired,

102

rabbity-looking girl who might work at Smedleys Electronics? I saw her with Smedley in Bath on Sunday. Smedley's been poisoned. It isn't anything to do with us any more but I'd really like to know who she is. And ask him about Fairy and Trixie. Evidently they were threatening to tell the school about him unless Jessica hung out with them. Also she was into something with them that she described as being just work."

"Will do."

Agatha rang off and asked, "What now?"

"What about, say, talking to Trixie's parents while we wait for the pair to get back from school?" said Phil.

"There's an idea. Let's go. Mrs. Freedman, could you find out about a bereavement class and phone the information to Mrs. Bradley? And is there any news from Harry?"

"Nothing. I'll find out about the bereavement class right away."

Agatha had expected Mrs. Sommers would prove to be a hard-faced blowsy woman, but it transpired she was small and meek and harassed-looking with pale blue eyes and neat hair.

"We are investigating the death of

Jessica," began Agatha, "and wondered if we might ask you a few questions."

"Come in. That poor girl."

The living room was almost a mirror image of the Bradleys': three-piece suite, coffee table, but no books.

When they were seated, Mrs. Sommers asked anxiously, "How can I help?"

"Jessica had a boyfriend, a much older boyfriend," said Agatha. "In a letter Jessica received from this boyfriend, it appears that Trixie and Fairy had told Jessica that if she didn't hang out with them, they would tell her teachers that she was going out with this man."

Agatha expected a hot denial, something on the lines of, "My daughter would never do a thing like that," but Mrs. Sommers looked sad. "I don't know what to do with my daughter, and that's the truth. My husband won't hear a word against her. He gives her too much pocket money and just laughs when I protest at her clubbing and wearing make-up. 'You're in the dark ages,' he says. 'Let her have her fun when she's young.' "

"So you think Trixie might have been blackmailing Jessica?"

"That's too strong. She might have teased her about it."

The front door crashed open. "Trixie?" called her mother. Trixie and Fairy sauntered in and stopped short at the sight of Agatha and Phil.

"What are you doing home from school so early?" asked Mrs. Sommers.

"Sports. We don't do sports," said Trixie.

"Is it true you threatened to tell Jessica's teachers that she was seeing an older man if she didn't hang out with you?" asked Agatha.

"Naw. Well, maybe we might have teased her a bit. We was friends. Wasn't we, Fairy?"

Fairy moved a wad of gum to the other side of her mouth and volunteered, "Yeah."

"Were you doing any sort of work with Jessica after school?"

They stared at her with flat eyes.

"Do you know of anyone who might have wanted to harm her?" pursued Agatha.

"Maybe her boyfriend."

"He has a cast-iron alibi. Anyone else? Boy at school?"

"Naw. She was crazy about her fellow. Said they was going to get married. Can we go to my room, Mum? This is boring."

They're old, so old, thought Agatha, with their flat, dead eyes. I wonder if they do drugs. I must ask Bill if that club has ever been raided.

"Run along," said Mrs. Sommers. She smiled weakly at Agatha. "It's all a front, you know. Trixie will soon grow out of it."

"Wait a bit," said Agatha to the girls. "Did you see her at the club the night she was murdered?"

"Sure," said Fairy. "She was there but she started rabbiting on about having to get home, so we left her to it."

With that, they both slouched out of the room.

"Didn't get much there," said Agatha outside. "Now what?"

"Maybe send young Harry back to the club this evening," suggested Phil. "He might be able to find out more."

Agatha made an appointment with Richard Rasdall, the masseur in Stow-on-the-Wold, for early evening. All her hip needed, surely, was a bit of massage. The massage room was in the bathroom above a sweet shop called The Honey Pot.

Lyn Rasdall, Richard's pretty wife, looked up from serving chocolates and said, "You know the way. He's waiting for you."

Agatha climbed up the steep stairs at the back of the shop where Richard was standing on the landing. He retreated while she stripped down to her knickers, covered herself with a large bath towel and climbed on the table.

When Richard came in, Agatha said, "I've got a little twinge of pain in my hip."

"Arthritis?"

"Of course not! I'm too young!"

"Can hit at any age. If I were you, I'd get that hip x-rayed. But let me see what I can do."

While he worked on her, Agatha told him about trying to find Jessica's murderer.

"It may turn out to be some stranger who just picked her up on the road," said Richard.

"I don't think she'd have got in a car with a stranger. Not these days."

"She was stabbed, wasn't she? She could have been forced to get in."

"With a gun, maybe. But a knife?"

"Maybe whoever it was saw her standing, waiting to cross. You said you didn't think she'd use the bridge at that time of night. He might have looked quite safe. Middle-aged. Gets out the car and says, 'Are you all right?' She replies that she's going home. He asks, 'Where's home?' She tells him. 'Funny thing,' he says, 'I just happen to be going that way. Hop in.' Was she murdered in the car?"

"I don't know."

"You should ask."

When Agatha left — pain in the hip gone, arthritis — rubbish! — she took out her mobile phone and called Bill Wong.

"Was Jessica murdered in a car? What do forensics say?" she asked.

"Looks that way. Not enough blood at the scene. She could have been murdered anywhere and then dumped. We're going on television tonight again to appeal to any driver who might have seen her."

"The other thing. Has Mrs. Smedley been accused of murdering her husband?"

"He was poisoned in his office. She was in the church in Ancombe all morning, cleaning the brass and doing the flowers. We've got nothing to hold her on."

"What about that girl I saw him with?"

"His secretary. She said her mother, who lives in Bath, was poorly, so he drove her over."

"Come on! What were they doing listening to the band?"

"We checked up. Mother is in a residential home in Bath. Yes, they did call on her. Maybe they decided to enjoy the sunshine. Relax, Agatha, it's not your case."

Agatha rang off and went home and fed her cats. Doris Simpson, her cleaner, had probably fed them earlier, but feeding them made Agatha feel less guilty for leaving them so much on their own.

She started to heat up her own dinner. And then she stiffened. There was the sound of movement upstairs. She looked wildly around for a weapon and seized a bottle of spray detergent. She stood at the bottom of the stairs. "Who's there?" she called.

"Me, Charles," came a voice. "Be down in a minute."

I'm going to take my keys away from him, vowed Agatha. He might have phoned to warn me he was coming.

She said as much when Charles pattered down the stairs.

He kissed her on the cheek. "Sorry. I'll phone next time."

"What happened to your gorgeous lady?"

"You'll never believe it."

"Try me."

"I was just moving in for the kill when

she pushed me away and said she couldn't because she had found God."

"Excellent," said Agatha cynically. "I must try that next time. What a put-down! I mean, there really is no answer to that."

"I haven't noticed men queuing up to get *you* into bed."

They were just glaring at each other when the doorbell rang.

Agatha went to answer it and found Mrs. Mabel Smedley standing on the doorstep.

"Come in," said Agatha.

She led Mabel into the kitchen. Charles wandered off into the sitting room.

"Coffee?"

"No, thank you."

"Please sit down. You must be very upset."

Mabel did not look upset. She was dry-eyed and composed. Agatha sat down opposite, reached for her cigarettes and then decided against smoking.

"It's like this," said Mabel. "My husband has been poisoned at work. The police have been questioning me all day — as if I had anything to do with it! I want you to find out who killed my husband."

"Very well," said Agatha. "I will get Mrs. Freedman to draw you up a contract. Now, did he have any enemies?"

"No, everyone loved Robert."

Agatha gave a little sigh. "Look, I do not want to add to your grief, but I cannot envisage everyone loving Mr. Smedley. I mean, someone must have hated him enough to poison him. Do they know how the poison was administered?"

"In his morning coffee."

"And who took him his coffee?"

"His secretary, Joyce Wilson."

"Does Joyce have red hair?"

"Yes."

"I saw Joyce with your husband in Bath last Sunday."

Did her eyes glint a fraction? But she said in an even voice, "Robert told me about that. Poor Joyce had been to visit her mother."

"So he wasn't having an affair?"

"Don't be ridiculous. He was devoted to me — so much so that he employed you to spy on me."

"And that didn't make you angry?"

"I thought it was rather sweet. Do you know there's smoke pouring out of your oven?"

"Blast!" Agatha shot to her feet and switched it off and then opened the back door to dispel the smoke. She normally microwaved her meals but had found that the lasagne she had bought for dinner was of the kind that needs to be cooked in the oven.

"Mrs. Smedley . . ."

"Mabel, please."

"Right, then, Mabel. My assistant noticed you had a bad bruise on your arm."

She gave a merry little laugh. Agatha was suddenly sure that merry little laugh had been well rehearsed. "I'm very clumsy. I'm always banging into things."

"We'll leave that for a moment. How do you wish me to start?"

"I own the company. I shall sell it, of course. I have told the staff to be prepared to be interviewed by you."

"I'll start with Joyce. Surely she is under suspicion since she gave him the coffee."

"No, she says she took a new jar out of the cupboard. It was instant coffee. He always took four lumps of sugar in his coffee and I think that must have been what masked the taste of the poison."

"I'll try to start tomorrow, but the police will be swarming all over the place."

Mabel rose to her feet. "I will leave you to it. Do your best. Robert's murderer must not go unpunished."

"Have you got Joyce's address?"

She opened her handbag and took out a

notebook. "I'll write it down for you." Agatha gave her a piece of paper and a pen.

"I might try her home tomorrow," said Agatha. "She might decide to stay away from work."

Agatha saw Mabel out and then went into the sitting room where Charles was sprawled in front of the television.

"This lack of curiosity is not like you."

"She made a bit of a fool of me, so I'm prejudiced. I listened at the door. She did it. Must have. All this business of 'Find the murderer of my husband' is just a blind."

"I don't know. I'll be interested to see what this Joyce has to say for herself."

"I'll come with you. I'm bored."

"I won't need photos. I'll phone Phil now and tell him to hitch up with Harry."

She dialled Phil's mobile. When he answered, she could hear thudding music in the background.

"Where are you?"

"At the disco with Harry."

"You'll stick out like a sore thumb!"

"They don't know I'm with him. I said I was taking photos for the local paper. The faces might come in handy."

"Can you go outside? I can barely hear you."

"Right."

She told Phil about Mrs. Smedley's visit, ending up by saying, "You and Harry work on the other cases tomorrow and tell Patrick to keep on the Jessica case and I'll talk to you tomorrow." She rang off.

"What's that terrible smell?" asked Charles.

"That was dinner."

"I'll phone out for a pizza. Don't feel like going anywhere."

"Me neither," said Agatha. "I can hardly wait to see what Joyce has to say for herself."

Six

The following morning, Charles and Agatha set out. "What kind of car is this?" grumbled Charles. "Here we are in the middle of global warming and you've bought a heap without air conditioning."

"It's a sturdy little car. Nobody's going to steal it or scratch it. It doesn't even have a CD, so they won't smash the windows to pinch the radio."

"I wonder if Joyce lives alone or with her parents?" mused Agatha. "Easier if she's on her own."

"Is she that young?"

"No, maybe getting on for thirty."

"*That* old," said Charles with a sideways malicious look at Agatha. He felt she was letting herself go these days, and although they did not have a romantic involvement, he thought she might have spruced herself up a bit. Her waistline had thickened and she had forgotten to put on any make-up. He couldn't remember Agatha ever forgetting to put on make-up before.

"Here we are," said Agatha at last. "Cherry Road. Quite near Jessica's home. I can't see a secretary affording a house even in this modest neighbourhood. Rats! She must be staying with her parents."

She stopped outside the house. "Here goes."

They walked up to the front door and rang the bell. Joyce Wilson answered the door. Her eyes were almost as red as her hair with recent weeping.

Agatha introduced them and said, "May we talk to you for a little?"

Joyce ushered them in. The living room was neat and tidy but strangely devoid of personality. New three-piece suite, low coffee table, television, mushroom-coloured carpet, mushroom-coloured curtains, and that was all.

"Have you lived here long?" asked Agatha and they all sat down.

"Not long," said Joyce, clasping and unclasping her thin fingers. "I rent it."

Wonder if the horrible Smedley paid the rent, thought Agatha.

"We were interested to know if you had any idea how the poison got into Mr. Smedley's coffee?" asked Charles.

She shook her head. "I opened a new jar and tore off the foil at the top."

"Did he take it black?"

"No, milk and a lot of sugar."

"What about the sugar? Lumps?"

"Yes. He always had four lumps in his coffee."

"Have the police suggested the poison might have been in the sugar?"

"They don't think so. Evidently it was a lot of poison and they don't think it could possibly have been inserted into the sugar lumps."

"What about the milk?"

"It's possible. There was just enough left in a bottle in the fridge. There was also a full bottle there. I used the little left and then I washed out the bottle with hot water and put it in the rubbish. The police tried to say that maybe the milk was poisoned and that I'd washed out the bottle to hide the evidence. But I didn't kill him! I didn't!"

Agatha took a chance. "How will you be able to afford going on living here now that Mr. Smedley isn't around the pay the rent?"

"I don't . . . he didn't . . ." She gasped and then burst into tears.

Charles saw a box of tissues on the coffee table and handed it to her. She sobbed and gulped and then blew her nose.

"I saw you in Bath with Mr. Smedley," said Agatha. "You were having an affair."

"It was just until he got a divorce," she said in a low voice.

"But he seemed devoted to his wife," Charles pointed out.

"He hated her," said Joyce with sudden venom. "I hated her. She was always turning up at the office and making catty little remarks in that sugary voice of hers. 'Not married yet, Joyce? We'll need to find you a husband. Won't we, Robert?' That sort of thing. Everyone thinks she's so perfect, but she's rotten underneath."

"How long had you been having an affair with him?" asked Agatha.

"Six months."

"But why?" asked Agatha. "He was a pompous middle-aged man."

"He was sweet to me. He took care of me!"

"Can you think of anyone who might have wanted him dead, apart from his wife?"

"I can't. He wasn't popular, but the men said the wages were good, so they put up with him. Can you go now? I've had enough. I've got to go back to the police station later for more questioning."

Agatha gave Joyce her card and asked

her to phone if she remembered anything significant.

When they returned to Carsely, it was to find Bill Wong waiting for them. "I've just heard from Mrs. Smedley that she's employed you to find out who murdered her husband. I warn you, Agatha, not to keep things from the police. You've done that in the past and nearly got yourself killed."

"Oh, come in and stop complaining," said Agatha. "It's too hot. I've ordered one of those mobile air conditioning units. Should be here this afternoon."

"That'll set you back a bit," commented Bill, following her into the kitchen where the cats leapt on him in welcome.

"Let's sit in the garden," said Agatha.

When they were seated over cups of coffee, Agatha said, "What sort of poison was it?"

"Weedkiller. He vomited most of it up and might have survived but he had a weak heart. He hadn't drunk all the coffee — just one gulp, but that was enough. Must have tasted bitter."

"Was there anything on his computer?" asked Charles. "I mean, there might be emails."

"Now that's the weird thing," said Bill.

"There was nothing but business affairs on the office computer, but his home computer had been wiped clean. So we took out the hard drive and ran it through that machine forensics has which can print stuff off the hard drive and it had been overwritten. You can buy a programme that overwrites everything."

"That points to the wife," said Agatha.

"Mrs. Smedley appears to know nothing about computers and the disc with the overwrite programme had only Smedley's fingerprints on it. He might have indulged himself by watching porn, maybe kiddie porn, and decided to wipe it out."

"Does Mrs. Smedley have any weed-killer?"

"None at all."

"I thought everyone had weedkiller."

"Not her. She goes in for organic methods. No chemicals. She's just what she seems, Agatha. She's a thoroughly nice woman. She even baked a batch of fairy cakes for us at police headquarters. She said that baking took her mind off her grief."

"You're a trusting lot," jeered Agatha. "She could have poisoned every single one of you."

"We're trying to find out more about

Joyce Wilson," said Bill. "But I can't see how it could have been her. I mean, she gave him the coffee. Surely a murderer would not make things look so obvious."

"We've just spoken to her," said Agatha. "She'd been having an affair with Smedley for six months and he was paying the rent of the house she's living in. She says he promised to marry her."

"Could be a bluff. He may have told her it was over."

"What about the factory?"

"We're currently interviewing all the staff. Then there's this Jessica murder. The press are hounding us for a result. I'd better go. Now, don't hide any clues."

He was about to leave when he hesitated on the doorstep. "Are you all right, Agatha?"

"Fine. Why?"

"You don't look your usual self."

"What's that mean?"

"Not as groomed as usual. And you aren't wearing make-up. I've never known you not to wear make-up before."

"Oh, just giving my skin a rest. See you. Bye."

As soon as he had left, Agatha nipped upstairs to the bathroom and stared in the magnifying mirror. She let out a squawk.

Her hair was limp, her skin was shiny and she had a spot on her nose. Worse, she could see the shadow of an incipient moustache on her upper lip.

She went downstairs and out into the garden where Charles was lying on the grass, playing with the cats. "I've got to go into Evesham," she said. "Could you be an angel and wait here and let the air conditioning man in?"

"Why Evesham?"

"Hairdresser."

Agatha spent a whole afternoon getting a facial, a seaweed wrap, and then her hair styled.

As she drove back to Carsely, she hoped the air conditioner had arrived. The air was like soup.

When she walked into her sitting room, she was greeted by a blast of cold air. "Great, isn't it?" said Charles from the depth of the sofa. He twisted up and looked at her. "Now, that's an improvement. What if James came back into your life and found you'd let yourself go?"

"Stop making personal remarks. I've an idea. Why don't we try to see Burt Haviland tomorrow?"

"Who's he? Remind me."

"Jessica's boyfriend. I'm clutching at straws but he may just want to help us."

"I thought Patrick and the others were following that case."

"Yes, but he might know someone at the factory who had it in for Smedley."

Agatha and Charles carried the mobile air conditioner up to Agatha's bedroom that night. "I'll leave my door open and you'll get the benefit, too," said Agatha.

Agatha undressed and got into bed. She fell asleep immediately and was awakened in the middle of the night by a crack of thunder. She fell asleep again and dreamed of Robert Smedley pursuing her across the icy wastes of the Antarctic. In her dream, she slipped and fell and awoke with a cry. Rain was lashing down outside and the room was like an icebox. Rain was drumming on the thatch and falling onto the garden in a series of waterfalls. She switched off the air conditioner, climbed back into bed and pulled the duvet over her head.

When she awoke again, it was to find the house was still cold. "Sodding British weather," muttered Agatha, turning on the central heating. "I should never have bought that air conditioner."

They set out to interview Burt Haviland after Agatha had called Patrick and found Burt was at home, having taken several days leave. The rain had become a thin drizzle and the day was cold.

"It's at times like this," said Agatha, "that I wish I'd never started a detective agency. I want to go somewhere warm and lie on the beach."

"I thought you'd have had enough of heat."

"Heat on the beach is different from heat inland."

They drove on in silence until they reached Burt's address. "Here we go again," sighed Agatha.

Burt Haviland was a very handsome man with thick black curly hair and a light tan. He must be paid well, thought Agatha, who had noticed the expensive motorbike outside and now saw that his living room contained a huge flat-screen television and a fancy computer.

Agatha explained that they were looking into the murder of Robert Smedley and asked him if he knew anyone at the factory who might have disliked him.

"Everyone hated him," said Burt. "But he paid good wages."

"Why did they hate him?"

"He was a bully. He liked finding out about people, finding their vulnerable spot, and pressing it."

"And yet they all stayed on?"

"All that I know of. I've only been with them two years. Oh, I think Eddie Gibbs left."

"Why?"

"His wife has muscular dystrophy and she's in a wheelchair. Smedley said to him with a sort of fake jollity, 'Must be hard on you not getting your leg over.' Eddie smacked him on the mouth."

"When was this?"

"About two months ago."

"Do you know where he lives?"

"Joyce'll know," said Charles. "I took a note of her number."

Agatha's mobile phone rang. It was Patrick. "You'd better get back here fast, Agatha. Harry's found something important."

"We've got to go," said Agatha. She turned in the doorway. "Is your name Burt Haviland? I mean, is that really your name?"

He turned red. "I changed it a few years ago."

"From what?"

"Bert Smellie. I got sick of people

making jokes about my name and my girl-
friend at the time picked a new name for
me out of a romance she was reading."

Outside, Agatha said, "We've got to get
back to the office, fast. Harry's found
something."

"You mean the one you told me was a
troglodyte with studs?"

"Yes, but he's bright."

Agatha burst into her office with Charles
at her heels. "What is it?" she demanded.
"What have you found?"

Harry went over to the computer. "I'll
show you. I was down at the cyber café to
send an email and this schoolboy was
staring at something on one of the screens.
I glanced over his shoulder and this is what
I saw."

He clicked on to the Internet and typed
in "hotsugarbabes. com." A picture flashed
up on the screen and Agatha bit back an
exclamation. There was a photo of Jessica,
Trixie and Fairy in their school uniforms.
"Now, you want to see more, you click
here and enter your credit card number.
What's yours?"

Agatha took out her card case and read
him out her Visa number. Another picture
came up.

It showed a film of Fairy, Trixie and Jessica lounging on a bed. They were all wearing lacy teddies and fishnet stockings. They giggled and pouted at the camera. Occasionally they kissed one another and fondled one another's breasts. "You want me to go on?" asked Harry.

"No, that's enough for now. Does it get worse?"

"Not really. There's a lot of them in school uniform — you know, blouses open to the waist and stocking tops."

"Goodbye, age of innocence," said Charles.

"I don't think any of them had the expertise to set up a Web site," said Harry.

Agatha remembered the expensive equipment in Burt Haviland's living room. "We'd better call the police on this one," she said. "I'll phone Bill."

Bill said he would be around right away. Agatha turned to Harry. "How does this work?"

"There are men who like looking at pictures of sexy schoolgirls. They pay up. It's usually safe enough for the girls because they never need to be in contact with their clients. Maybe one of them recognized Jessica at the roadside and got carried away."

"But it wasn't a sex crime," Charles pointed out.

The door opened and Bill Wong came in. "I hope you're not wasting police time. What have you got?"

Agatha silently pointed to the computer.

Harry flicked through the images for Bill. "Stop there!" said Bill suddenly. Agatha looked over Harry's shoulder. The three girls were in bikinis, chasing one another around a garden. Jessica seemed to be protesting and the other two pulled her hair and then dragged her to the ground.

"How did you get on to this?" asked Bill.

How Agatha would have loved to take the credit. "Harry," she said. "Tell Bill how you discovered this."

Harry did while Bill listened intently. Then Agatha said, "Burt Haviland has a lot of expensive equipment in his home. His real name's not Burt Haviland. It's Bert Smellie."

"We'll run that name through the computer. I'd better get a search warrant for his flat."

"Bill, remember we found this out for you and let us know how you get on."

"I'll try to get round tonight. You, Harry, come with me. I'll need to take a statement from you."

Bill and Harry left, and shortly afterwards Phil and Patrick came in. They told them about the computer video.

"Well," said Phil, "I was wondering why a nice girl like Jessica could go and get herself murdered in such a horrible way. Now we know. Could have been anyone."

"We'll get back out there," said Patrick. "We'll see Trixie and Fairy and tell them they've been found out. If the police have pulled them in, we'll try the parents."

When they'd gone, Charles said, "I'm going off for the afternoon, Agatha. Got things to do at home. See you later."

Agatha slumped down on the sofa. She felt tired and jaded. "Mrs. Freedman," she said. "You don't wear make-up? Does your husband ever ask you to?"

"No, m'dear. Doesn't notice much."

"Bill noticed when I wasn't wearing make-up."

"Could be a way of him saying you haven't been your usual sparky self lately. Have you eaten anything?"

"Haven't had time."

"Go out and get something. I'll look after things here."

"You're a treasure."

Agatha went out and round to a café and ordered sausage and chips, which she doused liberally with ketchup. She wished she could shake off the heavy feeling of nothingness that was beginning to overtake her.

She did not realize that the root of the problem was that she was obsessive when it came to men. Agatha was addicted to falling in love. While she was obsessing about some man, she could dream. But now, with no obsession, when she lay down to sleep at night there seemed to be a black hole left in her head, around the edges of which swirled nagging, petty little worries.

Charles was sitting at his desk going through the farm accounts when his man-servant, Gustav, announced, "Chap called Freddy Champion to see you."

Charles's face lit up. "Freddy! Haven't seen him in ages. Show him in."

A tall, lean, bronzed man with a shock of white hair and dark brown eyes came into the room.

"Out of Africa?" asked Charles.

"Thrown out of Zimbabwe."

"What will you do now?"

"Nigeria's offering us farmers land. Might try that."

"You're a devil for punishment." They talked of old friends and old times and

130

then Charles talked about Agatha and the murders.

"What an extraordinary woman she seems to be. I'd like to meet her."

"If you're not doing anything this evening, I'll take you over. Where's the missus?"

"Gone to South Africa for a break."

Agatha tried to work in her office at home that evening, writing down everything she knew about the Smedley case. The evening was cold and damp and she wished she'd never gone to the expense of buying an air conditioner. She switched off the computer. She had changed into an old pair of trousers and a sweater. No need to dress up for Bill and Charles.

She fed the cats but was reluctant to prepare anything for herself. Perhaps she and Charles could go to the pub after Bill had left.

The doorbell rang. When Agatha answered it, she found not only Charles standing there but a tall, handsome man. Charles introduced Freddy. Agatha was suddenly acutely aware of her old sweater and trousers.

Any minute now, thought Charles cynically, Agatha's going to say she's nipping up to the bathroom and she's going to come down with her face freshly made up. And that's exactly what Agatha did.

Agatha began to ask Freddy about his life in Zimbabwe. Charles, watching her animated face and sparkling eyes, suppressed a groan. He was just about to drop some remark about Freddy's wife when the doorbell rang announcing Bill's arrival.

"Well?" demanded Agatha eagerly.

Bill sat down at the kitchen table. He looked enquiringly at Freddy and Agatha quickly introduced him.

"We ran the name Bert, or Albert, Smellie through the police computer. I'm amazed he gave you his real name. How did you get on to that?"

"Think of it," said Agatha. "Burt Haviland is like one of those names in romance books."

"Anyway, he's got a record for armed robbery. In prison took his A levels. Left prison and took a degree in electronics engineering. Bright lad. His probation officer was so proud of him. We raided his house. We found the video set-up hidden in a shed in the garden. But we recognized his bedroom and the garden from the video. He blustered and protested that it was just a bit of fun. The girls weren't doing anything pornographic and it was an easy way to make money out of dirty old men. We're keeping him in overnight for more questioning and while we double-check his alibi for the night Jessica was killed."

"Did the parents know about this?"

"They were genuinely horrified," said Bill.

"Where did three schoolgirls get the time to do all this?"

"Weekends, evenings, school holidays. We're tracking down all the men who paid for a viewing."

"I've an idea," said Agatha, suddenly excited. "Maybe these two murders were tied up in some way. Robert Smedley's computer at home had been overwritten to conceal what he had been logging into."

"It's an idea. We'll check his credit-card details. I don't suppose we'll need a search warrant. Mrs. Smedley is very helpful. In fact, she's one of the most charming ladies I've come across in a long time."

"Humph," muttered Agatha. "But what about Burt? Is he still claiming he was madly in love with Jessica?"

"Yes, he is. He said the video thing was a bit of fun. He was saving up to give Jessica a super wedding."

"And you believe him?"

"I don't know what to believe and that's a fact. Thanks for the info, Agatha. We must have dinner sometime when all this is over . . . if it's ever over."

After Bill had left, Charles suggested they all go out for dinner. He watched uneasily as Agatha sparkled and told highly embroidered stories of her cases. He felt he should throw in some remark about Freddy's wife, but it was so grand to see Agatha once more back on form. Let Freddy tell her.

Freddy didn't, so Charles consoled himself with the thought that after this evening Agatha would probably never see him again.

But when Charles, predictably, went to the toilet as soon as the bill arrived, Freddy said, as he paid for it, "I have enjoyed this evening. I'm a bit at a loose end at the moment. What about dinner, just the two of us, on Saturday?"

Agatha glowed. "That would be lovely."

"Good. I'll pick you up at eight."

Freddy did not tell Charles of the arrangement he had made with Agatha, and Agatha did not tell him in case he volunteered to join them.

She went to bed that night wrapped in rosy dreams.

In the morning, at the office, Agatha said, "The police have talked to the parents, but see what more you can find out about this video business, Patrick, and take Phil with you. Did you see the girls?"

"No, the police chased us away."

"Harry," said Agatha, "you keep questioning her schoolmates. If a boy at the cyber café came across that Web site, then it stands to reason some of the others must have known what they were up to. Charles and I will try to track down Eddie Gibbs."

"Who's he?" asked Patrick.

"Some chap who left Smedleys Electronics. He evidently had every reason to hate Smedley. I know, we'll start with Joyce. I wonder if she's still at home."

Joyce was. Her face was very white against the red of her hair and her hands trembled. "Come in," she said. "The police asked dreadful things."

"What about?" asked Agatha.

"You'll never believe it. They wanted to know if he was keen on young girls. I was furious. Robert wasn't like that."

"We were wondering if you could find the address of a former employee called Eddie Gibbs."

"Oh, I remember him. A quiet little

man. Such a tragedy. His wife is in a wheelchair. I could look up the records in the office. I don't mind. I would like to get out for a bit in case the police come back. It's silly to go on hiding here. I'd better get back to work. I suppose Mrs. Smedley will sell the firm. Maybe the new people will keep me on. I'll get my jacket."

They drove her to the factory. Agatha wondered why Smedleys Electronics hadn't bothered to put in an apostrophe. Joyce shuddered a bit on the doorstep of the office.

"Fingerprint dust everywhere," said Agatha. "I thought they used a type of light or something."

"Do you think it's all right to touch anything?" asked Joyce.

"Sure," said Agatha. "The office door's no longer taped off."

Joyce hung up her jacket and sat down at the computer. She typed away busily and at last she said, "I've got it. Mr. Edward Gibbs, 78, Malvern Way."

"Where's Malvern Way?" asked Charles.

"It's over at the other end of Mircester on the Evesham Road. You take the dual carriageway and turn off at the second roundabout into Cherry Walk and Malvern Way is the third on the right."

"How do you know exactly where it is?"

"Eddie had a bit too much to drink at an office party and I drove him home."

"Did you ever hear him having a row with Mr. Smedley?"

"Well, yes," said Joyce awkwardly. "But Robert was very good about it. He said Eddie was all strung up because of his wife's condition."

They dropped Joyce back at her home and then set out to find Eddie Gibbs. "He'll be at work, won't he?" asked Charles.

"We'll have a word with the wife and find out where he is. Maybe catch him on his lunch break."

The house in Malvern Way was a small bungalow with a neat garden. Agatha rang the doorbell which played the Westminster chimes. The door opened and a woman in a wheelchair faced them. She had a long beautiful face, rather like one of the faces in a Modigliani painting.

"Yes?" she asked.

Agatha introduced them and explained they were trying to find out who had murdered Robert Smedley. She said they were anxious to speak to Mr. Gibbs.

"Why?" asked Mrs. Gibbs.

"Because he didn't like Mr. Smedley and

we thought he might give us a good picture of his character. The more you know about the murdered person, the easier it is to guess who might have wanted to kill him."

"Well, my Eddie wouldn't. He's too kind and nice. But come in. He won't be back until six this evening."

She wheeled herself back and they followed her into a sunny living room.

"Sit down," she said. Agatha and Charles sat down together on a sofa covered in cheerful chintz.

"I thought Smedley was a despicable man," she said. "He made several very crude remarks to Eddie about my condition. But his wife is a saint."

"You know Mrs. Smedley?" asked Agatha.

"I owe her a lot. She never said a word against her husband but she turned up here one day. Eddie had put his back out trying to get me to bed. She organized carers to come in the morning and get me up, give me a sponge bath and get me dressed, and to come in the evening to put me to bed. She organized Meals on Wheels to give me lunch and dinner, which means that Eddie has only got to pick up something for himself on the road home. That beast, Smedley, would not give Eddie a reference, but she wrote one out on the firm's paper and signed it on behalf of her husband."

"And where is he working now?"

"Over at Baxford Engineering on the Harley Industrial Estate. It's a good job and he's happy there. I know, he goes to Peg's Pantry at lunchtime, one till two. You can't miss it. It's the only restaurant on the estate. I don't know why we should help you with this because I'm glad he's dead."

"We won't bother you any further," said Charles.

"Is there any news about that poor girl who was also murdered, Jessica?"

"We're also working on that," said Agatha.

They drove to the industrial estate and waited until lunchtime before going into Peg's Pantry. "We should have asked for a photograph," mourned Agatha. "We don't even know what he looks like."

"I do," said Charles triumphantly. "When you were yakking on, I studied a photograph of him on the side table next to me."

"Good for you."

"Why are you looking suddenly uneasy?"

Agatha had in fact been wondering how to get rid of Charles on Saturday evening. But she said, "I was thinking about poor Mrs. Gibbs. I mean, people say if you're feeling down, find someone worse off than yourself. But all it makes me feel is that life can be terribly unfair. I think the sort of people who feel grateful at the expense of someone else's misfortune are the types in the old days who would have enjoyed a good hanging."

"Here he comes," said Charles.

A little man with small features and wispy hair had just entered the restaurant. He was wearing a checked shirt, an old tweed jacket, and jeans with knife-edge creases in them.

Charles rose and approached him. Agatha saw them talking and then Charles led Eddie over to their table.

He introduced Agatha and then said, "The least we can do is buy you lunch. What would you like?"

"I'll have sausage, egg, beans and chips and coffee."

Charles waved to the waitress and ordered the same for all of them.

"So why do you want to ask me about rotten Robert?"

"We believe you had reason to dislike

him," said Agatha. "No, we don't mean you murdered him. We mean, can you think of anyone in the firm who might have done it?"

Eddie shook his head. "A lot of us disliked him. Me, I hated him. But I can't think of anyone who would poison his coffee. Most of the men who disliked him would be more inclined to lash out with their fists. Poison is more a woman's thing, isn't it?"

"Only in fiction. Here's our food."

There was a silence while Eddie and Charles ate. Agatha pushed hers round on her plate. Normally she loved greasy food, but she didn't want to get spots before Saturday.

"So," said Eddie, "I don't think I can be of any help. Mind you, his wife's another thing. That woman's a saint."

"Your wife told us all she had done for you," said Agatha.

"Marvellous, she was. Did all the catering for the office party. Kind to everyone. Always a nice word."

"Fond of her husband?"

"Oh, yes. Devoted to the old bastard."

"Did you know," said Charles, "that Robert Smedley was having an affair with his secretary?"

"What, Joyce? I mean, why? What did she get out of it?"

"Her rent paid and probably a few presents. Besides, evidently Smedley told her he was going to get a divorce and marry her."

"So Joyce might have poisoned him. I mean, who else had the opportunity?"

"That's what we're trying to find out."

Agatha paid the bill and they thanked Eddie and left.

"Maybe we're being naive here," said Agatha as they drove off. "I mean, Joyce *is* the obvious suspect. Maybe she found out he didn't mean to marry her after all."

"And maybe," said Charles, "Mabel Smedley called on her and told her that."

"Good point. Let's go back and ask her.'"

Joyce was dusting the office when they arrived. "The factory is very quiet," said Agatha.

"Mrs. Smedley has told everyone to go home on full pay."

"When?"

"She called just after you left."

"Joyce, did Mrs. Smedley know about you and Mr. Smedley?"

"No, he was going to tell her after our weekend in Bath."

142

Charles said, "Say someone came during the night and got into the building and poisoned that bit of milk in the fridge. You've got CCTV cameras, haven't you?"

"Yes. That would be the job of Mr. Berry, in security."

"Where does he live?"

She switched on the computer. "I'll find his address for you. Here we are. He actually lives in Evesham, 4 Terry Road, near the tax office. Do you know where the tax office is?"

Agatha repressed a shudder. She had a good accountant but found the new complications of value added tax and staff pay bewildering.

Mr. Berry was digging in his small front garden when they drove up. Agatha, her mind full of Saturday night to come, left the introductions and explanations to Charles.

Berry was a burly man in blue overalls with a round red face and strands of grey hair combed across a bald spot on his head.

"We were wondering," began Charles, "whether the police found anything on the CCTV footage?"

"I ran the tapes for them before they took them away. Nothing but the staff

143

going to work and then leaving work. Nothing during the night but the night watchman."

"Who's the night watchman?"

"That'll be Wayne Jones, like. Lives over Worcester way."

"Do you know where in Worcester?"

"Might be in the phone book. I'll get it for you."

"I'm tired of all this running around," grumbled Agatha as they waited.

"We must persevere, Aggie."

"Don't call me Aggie." Agatha was beginning to fret. Charles was very keen and a keen Charles would certainly still be at her cottage on Saturday evening.

Mr. Berry came back with a slip of paper with an address written on it. "That must be it," he said. "His full name's in the book and he's the only Wayne Jones."

They went back to Agatha's car. She opened the boot. "I've got a pile of street directories here," she said, pulling a box forward. "I'm sure I've got one for Worcester."

She found the right map and looked up the address. "Right, got it," she said, pointing it out to Charles. "It's on this side of Worcester. You guide me."

"He must be a young man," said

144

Charles. "I mean, Wayne is a fairly new choice of name."

"Not that new now. I think it came in around the time Kylie became fashionable."

But when they ran Wayne to earth it was to find he was in his late twenties. He was tall and surly with a cadaverous face and deep-set eyes under a shaved head.

Again the introductions and explanations before Agatha asked, "Did you see anyone lurking around the night before Mr. Smedley was murdered?"

"All quiet. The police asked me that. What you lot mucking about for? It's their job."

"I told you," snapped Agatha. "Mrs. Smedley has employed us to find out who murdered her husband."

"And I'm telling you it was a night like any other. Now, piss off."

"He's on the defensive about something," said Agatha as she drove off.

"Probably went to sleep on the job."

"How do we prove that?"

"His patrolling should have been on the CCTV footage. Back to Berry."

Agatha groaned.

"Now what?" asked Berry, leaning on a spade, still in his front garden.

"Do you happen to know if the police studied the CCTV footage of the night before Mr. Smedley was murdered?"

"Yes, they did."

"And they saw Wayne on patrol?"

Berry grinned. "The silly sod was missing. Probably fell asleep. Forgot to tell you before."

"So anyone could have got past him?"

"The factory gates are locked and alarmed at night. There are cameras all over the place. Not a sign of anyone."

They thanked him and left. "Let's jack it in for the rest of the day," said Agatha. "We'll go back to the office and see how the others are getting on." But all the time she was wondering how she could get rid of Charles. Tomorrow was Saturday.

Freddy Champion was having dinner that night with old friends, Mr. and Mrs. Burkington-Tarry. He regaled them with stories of Charles and Agatha's investigation.

"We haven't seen Charles in this age," said Mrs. Burkington-Tarry. "We'll ask him to dinner."

"What about tomorrow night?" suggested Freddy. "I happen to know it's the one night he's free."

"What about this Agatha woman?"

"No, she works weekends."

Agatha was lying in the bath that evening wondering whether she ought to tell Charles the truth about her date with Freddy when the phone rang.

She heard Charles answer it but could not hear what he was saying.

She got out of the bath, dried herself and dressed and made her way downstairs. "Who was on the phone?"

"Old friends of mine. They want me to join them for dinner tomorrow night. You don't mind, do you?"

"Oh, no!" said Agatha.

"You mean you don't want me to go?"

"I didn't mean that at all," babbled Agatha. "Go, go, go!"

"All right. Calm down." Charles regarded her suspiciously. "Not up to anything, are you?"

"Me, no, of course not."

Seven

Agatha fretted all Saturday, wondering when Charles would leave so that she could begin preparing herself for the evening.

When he finally left at six o'clock, she hurtled up to her bedroom and started taking clothes out of her wardrobe. To her horror, after trying on a few of her best items, she found they were too tight at the waist. After agonizing for half an hour, she chose a black silk chiffon skirt with an elasticated waist and a white glittering evening top.

Just before eight, she was beginning to fret she was too dressed up. But when Freddy arrived promptly at eight, he was formally dressed in a dark lounge suit, silk shirt and striped tie.

"Would you like a drink before we go?" asked Agatha.

"Yes, please. Whisky and soda, no ice."

They went into the sitting room. Agatha was just preparing the drinks when the doorbell rang. "Maybe I shouldn't answer it," she fretted. "But maybe it's Bill Wong."

She went and opened the door. Mabel Smedley stood there. "I wondered how you were getting on," she asked.

"Come in," said Agatha reluctantly. She introduced Mabel to Freddy. "We're only a little further with the case," Agatha was beginning when Freddy interrupted.

"I heard about your sad loss," he said. "We were just going for dinner. Why don't you join us and Agatha can fill you in on the details?"

"That's very kind of you."

"Good, we'll take my car."

Agatha cursed under her breath. Freddy was relieved. His conscience, not usually active, was bothering him. Agatha was not a beauty and yet she exuded a strong air of sexuality which quickened his senses. He wanted to have an affair with her, but he was pretty sure Charles would let her know soon enough that he was married. Charles might even have already done so. Anyway, Mabel would be chaperone.

Over dinner in a restaurant in Broadway, Agatha forced down a resentment to Mabel — Mabel had taken the front seat in the car next to Freddy, leaving Agatha to sit in the back — and described what they had found out, with the exception of

Robert Smedley's affair with Joyce. She felt she would rather impart that bit of information when she was alone with Mabel.

Conversation then became general — or rather, it became general between Mabel and Freddy. Mabel, prim and proper in a navy wool dress, seemed to know a lot about Zimbabwe and the situation there and asked a lot of intelligent questions to which Freddy responded enthusiastically. Agatha sat practically ignored. It crossed her mind that Mabel might be cutting her out deliberately.

The meal ended. Freddy drove them back to Agatha's cottage and escorted Mabel to her car. Agatha said goodnight to Mabel, went into her cottage and slammed the door. A few minutes later the doorbell rang. Freddy smiled down at her. "You didn't give me a chance to say goodnight."

"Goodnight," said Agatha curtly. The door began to close.

"Look," said Freddy, "I was trying to help you by being nice to her. Let's have an evening by ourselves." He suddenly wanted to kiss Agatha as she stood, pouting slightly.

"Oh, all right. Just us. When?"

"Wednesday evening?"

"With Charles?"

"Without Charles."

"What will I tell him?"

"Tell him you're working on the case."

"That won't work. He'll wonder why I'm not taking him along. I know. There's a ladies' society meeting that evening. I'll tell him I'm going there."

"Good. He leaned forward to kiss her on the mouth, but Agatha drew back and said again, "Goodnight." She still had not quite forgiven him for spending the whole dinner talking to Mabel.

Agatha heard Charles coming home sometime after midnight but pretended to be asleep.

Bill Wong rang the next morning and invited Agatha and Charles to his home for Sunday lunch.

"It's an honour to be invited and I only accepted because of Bill," said Agatha. "How did he turn out to be so sweet with such awful parents? And he adores them. He never notices how rude they are."

Bill's father was Hong Kong Chinese and his mother was born in Gloucestershire.

Mrs. Wong, small, bent, sour, and fussy, opened the door to them. She jerked her head by way of greeting. They followed her

151

into the living room. Bill rose to welcome them.

The living room had been refurnished since Agatha had last seen it. There was a new three-piece suite covered in protective plastic, a low glass coffee table, a stuffed parrot on a perch by the window and a massive television set, all standing on a shag carpet of shocking pink.

"Where did the parrot come from?" asked Agatha.

"Great, isn't it? Dad picked it up at a boot sale."

Mrs. Wong came in with three small glasses of sweet sherry on an imitation silver tray which she banged down on the coffee table so that some of the sticky liquid slopped over the side. "Don't be long," she said.

Bill followed her out and came back with a roll of kitchen paper and the bottle of sherry. He mopped the tray and refilled the glasses.

They raised their glasses. "Cheers," said Charles.

The door burst open. "Don't sit there drinking all day," said Mrs. Wong. "Food's ready."

They hurriedly put down their glasses and followed her into the dining room.

The table was covered in a pink crocheted cloth. The knives and forks were imitation gold. Mr. Wong sat at the head of the table dressed in his usual old ratty grey cardigan. He grunted by way of greeting. His face was greyish yellow and he had a drooping moustache. Only his eyes behind thick glasses were like Bill's.

Soup was served, soup out of a can, tomato soup, Agatha's pet hate. But she was terrified of offending Bill's formidable mother, so she drank the lot of it. She tried to discuss the case, but Bill said gently, "Afterwards, Agatha. Mum doesn't like talking at the table."

"Yus," agreed Mr. Wong.

The next course was roast beef, cooked to the consistency of shoe leather, flanked by soggy potatoes, sprouts which had been boiled nearly to extinction and those canned peas which spread green dye all over the place.

Agatha chewed her way through the meal, glancing in amazement at Charles's plate. He had eaten everything in remarkably quick time.

She was the last to finish, aware the whole time of Mrs. Wong's beady eyes on her.

Mrs. Wong bustled round, collecting the plates.

"You're making a lot of extra work for Mother," commented Mr. Wong.

Agatha remembered her first visit to Bill's home, imagining delicious Chinese cooking.

Mrs. Wong jerked up the hatch from the kitchen and shouted, "Pudding. Hand round the plates, Bill."

Pudding turned up to be a piece of sponge cake in lumpy custard. Agatha gave up after a few mouthfuls. "I'm sorry, Mrs. Wong. I can't eat anymore."

"There's starving people in this world would be glad of that," said Mrs. Wong.

Inside Agatha's head, a voice screamed, "Then wrap it up and send it to them!" But she sat in silence with her head bowed like a child in disgrace.

At last the ordeal was over. "Go into the garden," said Bill, "and I'll bring the coffee out to you."

"It's raining," said Agatha, finding her voice.

"I've built a little conservatory," said Bill proudly. "Come and I'll show you."

He led the way out through the kitchen. But as he closed the dining room door, Agatha could hear the Wongs breaking into animated speech. Evidently the ban at speaking at the table only extended to visitors. What were they talking about? Probably complaining about me, thought Agatha.

The conservatory was a small room with a few potted plants and an iron table with chairs round it.

"Did you do all this yourself?" asked Charles.

"I did the foundations and the brickwork and then got a firm to do the rest. I'll go and get coffee. There's an ashtray on the table, Agatha. You can smoke."

No sooner had he left than Charles extracted a plastic shopping bag from the inside pocket of his jacket. He opened the door of the conservatory that led into the garden, whirled the bag round his head and sent it sailing into the garden next door.

When he returned, Agatha asked, "Was that lunch?"

"Yes."

"How did you do it?"

"Apart from Mrs. Wong glaring at you, Bill and his father never raised their eyes from their plates. So when they weren't looking, I took out the bag, opened it down between my knees and quickly tipped the plateful into it. I couldn't get rid of the pudding because I knew that wretched custard would stick to the plate. Shh! Here's Bill."

Bill came in with a tray of coffee things. Agatha lit a cigarette. "So what's happening?" she asked.

"We're checking up on all the men who paid to go into the girls' Web site. We examined Robert Smedley's records, just in case he was tied up with Burt in some way other than employer, and there was no sign of any payment."

"I find it hard to believe that the girls' parents knew nothing about what was going on."

"The parents are all pretty lax. We checked with the school. Most of the parents allow their kids too little supervision."

"There was one picture where Trixie and Fairy were pulling Jessica's hair and it didn't look like play. I think she was bullied into it."

"Probably did it out of love for Burt and was frightened of losing him if she didn't do what he wanted. How are you getting on with the Smedley case?"

"Nothing. Joyce would seem to be the obvious suspect. I mean, the weedkiller in, probably, the milk bottle. Although someone else could have got to that milk bottle before they packed up work on the Friday.

Even though she washed it, couldn't your forensic people still get something from the empty bottle?"

"We're still looking for it."

"What? Wasn't it in the trash?"

"Joyce said she always scalded out the empties with boiling water."

"Wait a bit," said Charles. "This doesn't add up. She pours his coffee, adds the milk, and takes it in to him. Don't tell me she then calmly stood in the little office kitchen scalding out the milk bottle while her boss was noisily puking up his guts next door."

"No. She says that because the kettle had just boiled for the coffee, she used the rest of the water to clean the bottle before taking the coffee in to him and left the bottle upended on the draining board."

"Why didn't you tell us about the missing milk bottle before?" asked Agatha.

"Because we didn't know it was missing. It now turns out that the Friday before, Smedley had a conference with several of the staff and they had coffee and biscuits. A bottle of milk and most of another bottle was used up, because two of the staff refused coffee and said they would each have a glass of milk instead. Joyce put the bottle with the little bit of milk in it in the fridge, scalded out the other one, and left it in the

157

kitchen trash. She could be lying, of course. But we haven't any proof. We've searched all the outside rubbish bins. There were milk bottles in some of them. We tested them all. The staff have all been fingerprinted. But we knew we were looking for two that had been cleaned. Couldn't find one."

"But who else could have had a chance to take the bottle away?"

"Joyce said when she heard Smedley dying, she screamed and screamed and everyone came running. It *would* be the one place that still has their milk delivered in bottles. The milk comes from an old-fashioned dairy in Gloucester."

"Did you tell Mrs. Smedley that her husband was having an affair with Joyce?"

"Yes. She says she knew nothing about it."

There came a hammering from the front door of the house and then the sounds of an angry altercation.

"I'd better go and see what's happening," said Bill.

"The food you threw into the neighbour's garden," said Agatha. "I bet that's what it's about."

"Let's run away."

"We can't."

"Think of the fury of Mrs. Wong."

They ran down the garden from the conservatory and out into a field at the back.

"My car's parked a little way down the road," panted Agatha. "I think we can reach it without Bill seeing us."

They climbed over a fence at the side of the field and down a lane which led to the front of the houses.

"Right!" said Agatha. "I've got the keys ready. Let's run for it."

But as they reached the car, Bill Wong emerged from the other side of it and stood with his arms folded.

"You're a disgrace!" he said. Agatha had never seen him so angry.

"It's my fault," said Charles. "I think I've got an ulcer. I didn't want to hurt your mother's feelings."

"You have not only hurt her, you've humiliated her."

"We'll go back and apologize," said Agatha.

"No, go on your way. I'm sick of the sight of you."

Agatha drove off. A tear began to roll down her cheek, followed by another.

"Hey!" said Charles. "Stop the car. I'll drive."

They changed places and Charles drove

off. "He was my first friend," sobbed Agatha.

"We'll stop in Mircester and send the old bat some flowers and a note of apology."

"Won't work." Agatha suddenly brightened. "But I know what might. Stop in the main square outside police headquarters. There's something in a shop down The Shambles which has something that might do the trick."

"Surely it won't be open on Sunday."

"Some of the shops are open. I think this one will be."

"You mean *that?*" asked Charles fifteen minutes later as they both stood looking in a shop window.

"She'll love it," said Agatha. "Trust me."

What so horrified Charles was a cylindrical plastic floor lamp in which golden bubbles rose and fell along with tiny plastic sea horses in jewelled colours.

They went into the shop and Agatha explained she wanted to buy it and have it delivered immediately.

"I haven't anyone to deliver it today," said the sales assistant.

"I tell you what; just wrap it up and give me a gift card. I'll send it out in a taxi."

Agatha paid while Charles wrote a card of apology. They carried the box with the lamp in it over to the taxi rank and paid a driver to take it to Bill's home.

"I hope you know what you're doing," said Charles. "That lamp might turn out to be adding insult to injury."

"Let's go and visit Mrs. Bloxby. Haven't seen her in a while."

They saw Mrs. Bloxby walking along the main street, stopped the car and hailed her.

"How are you getting on?" asked the vicar's wife. "I was just going home for a cup of tea. Care to join me?"

"Get in the car," said Charles cheerfully, "and we'll all go together."

In the vicarage sitting room, while Mrs. Bloxby went to fetch tea, Agatha relaxed and looked around her. She could never quite understand why Mrs. Bloxby's shabby sitting room should have such peaceful charm compared to her own. Everything was worn and parts of the silk cushions on the sofa were showing signs of splitting. There was a small round table by the window holding a blue jug of wild-flowers and bits of chipped antique furniture in corners of the room. But somehow it created a harmonious whole.

Mrs. Bloxby came back with the tea things and a plate of shortbread. "How is this business about Mr. Smedley's murder going?" she asked.

Agatha proceeded to tell her everything they had found out. When she had finished, Mrs. Bloxby said, "I don't somehow think it could have been this secretary."

"Why?"

"I cannot think anyone would have made themselves such an obvious suspect."

"We're going round and round in circles. Aren't you shocked about the schoolgirls' video games?"

"I don't think anything shocks me any more," said Mrs. Bloxby sadly. "The last time I went to the hairdresser, I had forgotten to take a book. There was a pile of magazines meant for girls in their early teens. They were all about sex. Quite disgusting. I think this Burt put them up to it and they thought it a bit of a lark."

"If Joyce isn't the culprit, surely Mrs. Smedley might be. She says she didn't know Robert was having an affair with Joyce, but I am sure she must have known there was something going on."

"Not necessarily. And how is your detective friend?"

Agatha let out a strangled sob. "I don't think he's a friend any more."

"Why? What happened?"

"It was Charles's fault." Agatha plunged into a description of what had happened at the dreadful lunch.

When Agatha had finished, Mrs. Bloxby put a handkerchief to her mouth. "Excuse me." She fled out of the room. They heard muffled sounds coming along the corridor.

"Is she ill?" asked Agatha. "Should I go to her?"

"I think she's laughing."

"Laughing? I've just lost my one best friend and she's laughing?"

Mrs. Bloxby came back into the room. Agatha did not notice that Charles's eyes had become suddenly cold.

"I am sorry," said Mrs. Bloxby. "But it really was so funny."

Agatha stared at her and then slowly began to giggle. "I suppose it is."

Charles rose to his feet. "If you ladies will excuse me. I've just realized, Agatha, that I have been neglecting things at home. No, don't get up. I'll walk back."

He went out, slamming the door. "What's the matter with him?" asked Agatha.

"Did you say anything when I was out of the room?"

"Let me see. I could hear sounds and I asked Charles if I should go to you. He said he thought you were laughing. I couldn't see the funny side of it just then. That's all. Maybe he has just remembered something urgent. I'm tired of murder. Tell me the parish news."

"Miss Simms — I think she will always be Miss Simms to me — is getting a divorce from Patrick."

"They said nothing to me!"

"Probably didn't want any fuss. It's by mutual agreement. Both of them thought they wanted to settle down. Patrick found it didn't suit him. I think our Miss Simms missed her casual affairs."

Agatha felt she should phone Charles that evening and ask him why he had decided to leave so suddenly. But an absent Charles meant a Charles who would, hopefully, not be around on Wednesday evening. She fed her cats and then switched on her computer and began to look up everything she could on Zimbabwe. She was just printing off some pages when the phone rang.

She answered it, expecting it to be

Charles, but it was Bill Wong. "You're a bad girl, Agatha, but really, Mum is over the moon about that magnificent present. She and Dad just sit there looking at it."

"I can only repeat how sorry I am."

"It was really Charles's fault. I've got this girlfriend, Harriet, a policewoman. I phoned her up and told her what Charles had done and how the pair of you had run away. She laughed and laughed and then she said my mum's cooking was awful. I never noticed. Is it?"

"It's a bit of an acquired taste. Oh, Bill, I am so glad we are friends again."

"Well, keep safe. And if you find a murderer, don't go tackling him on your own."

Agatha found it hard to get to sleep that night. Instead of concentrating on alibis for the morning of the murder, everyone should have been concentrating on the period from Friday until Monday. Anyone could have got in and poisoned the milk. But how would anyone get in unobserved with cameras all over the place and the gates locked?

Burt Haviland. Now he was the one with a criminal record. She resolved to go and see him the following day and take Phil with her. There might just be a connection between the two murders.

Agatha was grateful to Mabel Smedley for having suspended the staff from work. That way she had a chance of finding the ones she wanted to talk to at home. There was no reply at Burt Haviland's home, so she and Phil decided to wait outside in the car.

"It's a funny business, the Internet," mused Phil. "It's so useful for research and yet everyone has easy access to porn. Now although what the girls were showing could be classified as soft porn, it's still one more thing to corrupt the young. Even their figures have changed. In my youth, they stayed very slim and nearly flat-chested right up until they started work, but now they've got busts and backsides starting around the age of eleven years. Then they either start dieting ferociously or become as fat as anything. Not to mention the terrific rise in sexually transmitted diseases."

Agatha winced. She was mentally planning to start an affair with Freddy. But these were difficult days. No more tumbling carefree into bed. Always wondering if the sexual partner was really some sort of diseased time bomb.

"Oh, here he comes," said Phil.

Burt Haviland was walking along the street carrying a grocery bag. They both stepped out of the car.

"Oh, it's you," he said. "Haven't I enough to put up with having the police in my face all the time?"

"Just a few questions," said Agatha.

He leaned against her car. "Fire away. I'm not asking you inside."

"Who has the keys to the factory?"

"The security man. He opens up and locks up. Smedley would have had a set."

"Look, we're not accusing you of anything," said Phil. "But is there any way anyone could get into the factory without keys, say at night?"

"Well, there is. Berry was sometimes too quick off the mark at locking up. One of the men found himself locked in one night. He managed to get out through a fire door, but he couldn't find Berry anywhere. He walked round the perimeter fence and found a bit where the chain fence was loose at the bottom and prised it up and slipped through."

"Wasn't it electrified?" asked Agatha.

"No, the current only goes through the main gate. Word got around, but no one told Smedley or Wayne. We all wanted to think there was a way of getting out if the silly bugger locked anyone in again."

"Where could Wayne have been when this man was searching for him?" asked Phil.

"Don't know. He evidently wasn't in his office, which is just by the main gate."

"And can you show us where this bit in the fence is?"

"Find it yourselves," snarled Burt. "I'm sick of you."

"May as well try," said Agatha as they drove towards the factory. "What on earth was Mabel doing by suspending Berry from work? Anyone could raid the place."

"Maybe she's already got rid of any stock."

"So quick? I shouldn't think so."

They reached the factory and parked and then began to walk around the perimeter fence. Agatha would have walked right pass the spot because she was dreaming about Freddy, but Phil suddenly cried, "Here it is. Look down. You can see where the grass has been flattened." He bent down and tugged hard at the bottom of the fence and bent the chain link upwards. "There! That's how it could have been done. Let's go inside and have a look."

"Must we?" pleaded Agatha. She was wearing a yellow linen suit and the grass was wet.

"We've come this far. I would like a look at the office door to see if it's got the sort of lock that could be easily picked."

He got down on the ground and rolled through to the other side. "Come on, Agatha. It's easy."

Agatha tried but got stuck halfway and Phil had to force the fence up even higher.

She stood up and tried to brush herself down. Her suit was wet and smeared with green grass stains.

They had just got halfway towards the buildings when an alarm went off and two security men with Alsatian dogs straining at the leash came running towards them.

"Stop!" called one. "Or we'll let the dogs loose."

They both stood frozen to the spot.

"You will come with us," said one of them, "while we phone the police."

"We're employed by Mrs. Smedley to investigate the murder of her husband," said Agatha. She fished in her handbag and brought out her business card. "Phone her."

He studied the card and then took out a

mobile phone. He was wearing a black uniform with a badge on the front which said "Mircester Security."

While the other man stood guard, he walked a little away and began to talk into the phone.

At last he came back to join them. "Mrs. Smedley agrees she employed you, but says you had no right to break into the factory. You can go. Back the way you came and let me see how you got in."

They led the guards to the vulnerable bit of the fence. "We'll get that nailed down. Off you go."

"Can't you let us out the front gate?"

"Just go."

They rolled through one after the other. Phil helped Agatha up. Her hip gave a ferocious twinge and she let out a gasp.

"Are you all right?" asked Phil. "Got rheumatism?"

"No, just a cramp," said Agatha. "We'd better go and see Mabel Smedley and find out why she laid off Berry. Maybe she suspects him. I'll drop off at home first and change my clothes."

Mabel received them graciously and offered them tea. Agatha looked around the living room for clues but all she could see was a pleasant room with tasteful furniture and some very good paintings on the walls.

When Mabel had poured them excellent cups of coffee and offered home-made biscuits, she said, "All you had to do was tell me you were going to the factory."

"We found there was a way of getting through the fence. Burt Haviland told us. We wanted to see if the lock on the office door would be easy to pick. Because you had laid your security man off, we didn't expect anyone to be there."

"I hired a private security firm."

"Why?"

"I never quite trusted Berry. I think he drinks. I thought it safer to suspend everyone and if the new owners want to keep them on, that's their business."

"Have you found a buyer?"

"My lawyers are working on it. It's only a small factory, but profitable. It should not be on the market for long. I shall of course tell the new owners about Burt Haviland and those schoolgirls. The police told me about that. I was shocked. Pity. Burt was a very good salesman."

"I'm sure you won't be giving Joyce Wilson a reference."

"I find it hard to believe that Robert should have had an affair with that silly girl. The police told me about it. More coffee?"

"It must make you very angry."

"Robert is dead," she said with quiet dignity. "I am grieving. Getting angry doesn't help."

"Of course," said Phil with quick sympathy. "These biscuits are amazingly good."

"Have some more, do."

"Would you say the office lock could have been easily picked?" asked Agatha.

"It's just a Yale. The bit with all the electronic components was always securely locked."

"Maybe nobody needed to break into the factory," said Agatha. "Mr. Smedley had a meeting on the Friday. There was just enough milk left over for the Monday. But he wouldn't have coffee first thing because that was the morning you both came to see me."

"I went home and he went straight back to the office. He would automatically ask Joyce to fetch him a cup of coffee."

"Do you suspect Joyce Wilson?"

"Not for a minute. She's too spineless. Not the type."

When they had left, Phil said, "If you don't mind, I think perhaps we should be trying harder to find out who murdered Jessica. She didn't deserve to die. But Smedley did. You said he beat his wife."

"I think he did. I really could do with something to eat. Those biscuits gave me indigestion." Agatha was lying. She had only eaten one delicious biscuit, but she was tired of the fact that all the men around her seemed to dote on Mabel Smedley.

Eight

For the next two days, Agatha worked hard interviewing as many of Smedley's staff as she could find while Patrick and Phil worked on Jessica's murder. She was glad she had employed Harry, who seemed to be coping well with two divorce cases. Agatha was beginning to wonder if she could tempt him to forget about university and work for her full-time.

Charles was still absent. She had put him to the back of her mind because she wanted to have dinner alone with Freddy. But as she was driving home on Wednesday, she suddenly remembered with horror that at Mrs. Bloxby's she had said something about Bill being her only best friend. Charles had accused her before of having a selfish, cavalier attitude to her friends. She would phone him and make amends. But not until the next day.

Agatha, dressed in a very short skirt and a black jersey top and high heels, began to feel excited as she waited for Freddy to arrive. Just as he was ringing the doorbell, her telephone rang. She decided to ignore it.

Freddy planted a warm kiss on her cheek. "You look great," he said.

He took her to the same restaurant as before and asked her all about the case. Agatha launched into a description of all she had found out, quite forgetting she had meant to ask him all about Zimbabwe.

When she had finished, he gazed into her eyes and said, "You really are amazing, you know."

Agatha dropped her eyes, the lashes heavy with black mascara, in mock modesty and murmured, "Oh, I wouldn't say that."

"But you are! All this murder and mayhem. You must be very courageous."

Agatha remembered that she should be asking him about Zimbabwe, and asked, "Did you have an awful time in Africa?"

"It was pretty grim. A gang charged the farmhouse. They'd already killed most of my workers. We got out the back way just in the nick of time with only what we were wearing."

"We?" asked Agatha.

"I mean, me and my houseboy. It's a terrible situation. Because Mugabe has driven off all the farmers, the harvests are rotting in the fields and the country is starving. Oh, that reminds me. I'm leaving tomorrow for a short break."

Agatha's face fell. "For how long?"

"Just a couple of weeks."

"Let's hope I have these cases cleared up before you get back. Where are you going? Not back to Zimbabwe, I hope."

"No, I'm going to see, er, friends in South Africa. But I'll see you as soon as I get back. Anyway, let's make the most of our evening together." His eyes looked long and steadily into hers and Agatha got the unsaid message — the night as well.

That was when a little twinge of panic assailed Agatha. She had shaved her legs the day before, but she really should have gone for a wax. The evening was humid and she nervously imagined she could feel hair sprouting through the sheerness of her black stockings. It was a while since she had found the courage to look at her naked body in a full-length mirror. Then, what if he didn't have a condom? She didn't have any.

But she fought down her worries. Here was the most attractive man she had come across in ages. Maybe they would get married. But if they got married and he went out to Nigeria to farm, she would need to go with him.

So she drank more than she should to drown the worries and was feeling muzzy and relaxed when she got in the car for the drive to her home.

If I'm not meant to do this, she told herself, something will happen.

"Coming in for a nightcap?" asked Agatha.

"Of course."

He went round and opened the car door for her and helped her out. Agatha opened the door and reset the burglar alarm.

"I'll just let my cats in from the garden," said Agatha, suddenly nervous again. "Help yourself to a drink and make me a gin and tonic."

Agatha let her cats in and patted them.

He appeared behind her, making her jump. "Do we really need a drink?" he asked.

Agatha turned to face him. He cradled her face in his hands and bent his head to kiss her.

And at that very moment, sharp and shrill, the doorbell rang.

"Don't answer it," he murmured.

The doorbell rang again. "Police! Open up!" cried a voice.

Freddy drew back, looking alarmed.

Agatha rushed to the door and opened it. Detective Inspector Wilkes stood there, flanked by Bill Wong and a policewoman.

"Come in," said Agatha. "What's up? Is this going to take long?"

"All night if necessary."

Freddy, who had followed Agatha to the door, said quickly, "I'd better take myself off."

"Who are you?" demanded Wilkes.

"A friend of Agatha's. We've just had dinner. I'll be on my way."

"No, you don't. You'll stay until we get your address and what you were doing today."

"What's all this about?" asked Agatha as they all sat round the kitchen table.

"All in good time," said Wilkes ponderously.

"Oh, for heaven's sakes," snapped Agatha. "You've been watching too many cop movies. What's happened?"

"Burt Haviland has been found murdered."

"What! How?"

"Stabbed to death in his flat. A vicious assault. We'll start with your friend here. Have you been helping Mrs. Raisin on her cases?"

"No," said Freddy. "I'm just a casual friend."

"And where do you live?"

"I've just come over from Zimbabwe. I'm staying with a friend in Chipping Norton at the moment."

"Name and address?"

"Captain John Harvey, Orchard Farm. It's on the Oxford side of Chipping Norton."

"Married?"

"No," said Freddy.

"And were you with Mrs. Raisin earlier today?"

"No. I picked her up for dinner at eight o'clock. We went to the Feathers restaurant in Broadway. We'd just got back when you arrived. May I go now?"

"Yes, that'll be all right."

Freddy threw Agatha a guilty look and hurried out.

"When was he found?" asked Agatha.

"At six o'clock."

"And who found him?"

"We did. He dialled 999 before he died. Why didn't you answer your phone?"

"I was out. I wanted a quiet evening, so I switched off my mobile as well."

"When did you last see Burt Haviland?"

"Monday."

"What did you talk about?"

"I asked him if there was any way anyone could sneak through the fence and into the factory. He said there was a loose bit in the chain-link fence. So me and Mr. Witherspoon found it and slid through. We were heading for the office to study the lock and see if it was an easy one to pick. Mrs. Smedley had hired a firm of security guards and we were caught and sent off. That was the last time I talked to Burt and it was about the fence. You don't suspect me, surely? I was still in the office at six o'clock, finishing up business."

"I suspect you of withholding information."

"That's not true," said Agatha hotly. "I was the one who told you about the girls' Web site. Didn't the neighbours see or hear anything?"

"It's a small block of flats. They were all still out, apart from an old lady on the top floor flat who's stone-deaf."

"Well, I'm not withholding a damned thing and you've buggered up my date."

"Not a very gallant date," murmured Bill Wong. "Rushing off like that and leaving you to face the music."

"Right," said Wilkes. "We want you to report to police headquarters tomorrow at ten in the morning and we'll take a state-ment. You will tell us everything you know about Burt Haviland."

"But I already have!"

"Don't argue. Be there."

"When he was phoning for help, didn't Burt say who had stabbed him?"

"No. He said, 'I'm stabbed. Burt Havi-land. Send help,' and then the phone went dead."

After they had left, Agatha sat feeling miserable. Another murder. She was use-less as a detective and useless as a woman. Then she remembered Charles.

She phoned his number. Gustav an-swered the phone. Agatha asked for Charles. "He's busy," said Gustav rudely and put down the phone.

Agatha glanced at her watch. It was only eleven o'clock. She locked up again and got into her car. Driving carefully and hoping she would not be stopped and breathalysed, she arrived at Charles's man-sion and knocked on the door.

Agatha was prepared to battle her way past Gustav, but it was Charles himself who answered the door.

"Oh, it's you," he said. "What's up?"

"I'm so sorry, Charles," said Agatha.

"When I said that tactless thing about Bill being my best friend, I meant he was my first friend."

"You mean you didn't have any friends when you were working in London?"

"No," lied Agatha. "I meant he was my first friend when I moved to the Cotswolds. I'm sorry."

"Come in. Gosh, we do behave like kids sometimes. But you have been pretty off-hand with your friends in the past. Come through to the study."

"Burt Haviland's been murdered, stabbed to death."

"When?"

"Late afternoon. Six o'clock."

"How can the police be so precise?"

"He dialled 999 just before he died."

"Found the weapon?"

"I was so shocked I didn't ask."

"Drink?"

"No, I've had enough already. I shouldn't really be driving. The police called on me when I got home."

"So you've been drinking and you're all glammed up. What have you been up to?"

Agatha did not want to tell him about Freddy because she might lose Freddy, and that meant losing a dream and she was short on dreams.

"The ladies' society meeting."

Charles looked cynical. "All that for a bunch of women?"

"You're behind the times. Women dress up for other women. Anyway, I'm feeling pretty rotten. Three murders and I still haven't a clue about any of them. I'm due at police headquarters in the morning."

Agatha stifled a yawn.

"You'd better go home," said Charles. "I'll call for you at police headquarters. What time do you think they'll let you out?"

"Knowing the way they go on, I should think about noon. I'm due there at ten and they'll probably keep me waiting and then grill me over and over again."

"They can't force you to. You're not under arrest."

"I'd better do it. Can't start getting on the wrong side of the police."

"Right," said Charles. "I'll be waiting for you in reception."

Agatha drove steadily and carefully home. When she got out of the car and stood fishing her house keys out of her handbag, she suddenly stiffened. She had a feeling of being watched. She slowly turned round.

The cobbled lane was deserted. The lilac

trees from which it took its name rustled in the lightest of winds.

I'm tired, that's all, she told herself firmly. She let herself in and went up to bed. The cats followed her upstairs and stretched out on the bed. I really should stop them doing that, thought Agatha. She experienced a feeling of unease when she remembered how Freddy had cleared off. Charles would never have done that. But she needed her dreams, and by the time she fell asleep Freddy had once more been restored in her mind to the status of future husband.

The questioning was every bit as wearying as Agatha had expected it to be. Unlike previous cases, she held nothing back, feeling there was nothing to *hold* back, although at one point she guiltily remembered those letters Burt had written to Jessica.

It was with a feeling of relief that she found Charles waiting for her. Dear Charles. Always so loyal, thought Agatha, quite forgetting that Charles had happily dropped her in the past whenever a pretty girl came into his life.

"I'll phone everyone and get them all into the office," said Agatha. She took out her phone and while Charles waited, told everyone to head for the office. She rang off after the last call and said, "We need to plan some sort of strategy. Where's your car?"

"Off to the garage with Gustav. Something up with it. I've been thinking of something," said Charles.

"What?"

"Phil, despite his age, is a likeable and attractive man."

"I hadn't noticed," said Agatha huffily, wondering if Charles was trying to set her up with this geriatric.

"Well, he is. And has Joyce Wilson ever met young Harry?"

"No, where's this going?"

"Mabel knows Phil's on the case, so it would be natural for him to call on her, maybe get close to her. She may know more about her husband's enemies than she's told us. Joyce hasn't met Harry, has she?"

"No, I don't think so."

"If he could shed some of his studs and smarten up a bit, he could maybe ask her out. Now that one, I am sure, knows something. You told me about the missing milk bottle. Before the forensic team arrived, it would be easy for Joyce to hide it somewhere and dump it afterwards."

"Do you think she did it? I thought you had Mabel down as first murderer."

"She is the obvious suspect."

"What about Jessica's murder? And Burt? Surely they're tied up?"

"Think about it. Wouldn't it be better to concentrate all the forces on dealing with one murder at a time? The newspapers are still putting the police under pressure over Jessica's murder, so they'll still be concentrating all their efforts over solving that one, and Burt's as well."

"All right. We'll try it your way. I'll tell them."

"And no doubt take all the credit for having thought of it," murmured Charles, but Agatha pretended not to hear.

Later that day, Harry, with not a stud or earring in sight, and dressed conservatively in a soft brown suede jacket, Tattersall shirt and tailored slacks, sat in his parents' Audi at the end of Joyce's street. His parents were well-to-do, and as Harry was their only child, they indulged him with a generous allowance.

He knew there was a supermarket nearby, within walking distance, and hoped Joyce would go there. But she came out of her house at last and got into a battered Mini parked outside and drove off.

Harry followed. Joyce drove into the centre of Mircester and parked. Harry parked as well and followed her at a discreet distance. She went into the Abbey Tea Rooms. Harry waited a few minutes and went in as well. The tea room, famous for its cakes, was crowded. Joyce was sitting at a table in the corner by herself. There were no empty tables. Blessing his luck, Harry approached Joyce. "Do you mind if I sit here? Seems to be the only seat."

"No, go ahead," said Joyce. The waitress came up. Joyce ordered a pot of tea and a slice of carrot cake and Harry ordered coffee and a toasted teacake. He knew he would have to go carefully. Joyce had taken out a paperback romance and started to read, so he unfolded the newspaper he had originally bought to hide behind when he was watching her house, and pretended to read.

The waitress came up with their orders. Now what? Harry had thought of spilling his coffee on her as a way to break into conversation but rejected the idea almost immediately. All that would do would make her furious.

The table was very small. Joyce's tea was served in one of those metal pots that always seem to pour anywhere but in the cup. Her saucer filled with tea and she gave an exclamation of dismay.

Harry summoned the waitress with an imperious wave of his hand. "The young lady's teapot is not pouring properly. Please get her a good one."

"Oh, thank you," said Joyce. "But you really shouldn't have bothered."

Harry smiled. That smile he used so rarely but when he did, it lit up his face. "Least I can do for a pretty lady."

Then, so that he wouldn't appear so pushy, he picked up the paper again.

When her new pot of tea and clean cup and saucer arrived, he lowered his paper and said, "Allow me." He reached over and deftly poured a cup.

"Thank you," said Joyce.

Harry began to drink his coffee and eat his toasted teacake. Let her make the first move, he told himself.

Then Joyce spoke. "Are you new to Mircester?"

"No, I live with my parents out on Bewdley Road."

Joyce was impressed. She knew Bewdley Road. That was where the most expensive villas in the town could be found. Her eyes took in the expensive suede jacket.

"It's odd to find a young man living with his parents these days."

"I'm taking a gap year before I go to university," said Harry. He had decided not to try and cover up his age. Joyce would probably be flattered that a young man was interested in her.

He was about to pick up the paper again, but Joyce's curiosity had been awakened. She noticed he was wearing a Rolex. Joyce was attracted by any show of wealth.

"And what are you doing in your gap year?" she asked.

"I'm doing freelance computer programming work."

"And will you do that when you leave university?"

"Maybe. I'll be studying physics."

Joyce let out a sigh. "I wish I'd gone to university instead of being just a secretary."

"Where do you work?"

"Smedleys Electronics."

Harry let his eyes widen. "Good heavens! Wasn't there a murder there?"

"My boss." Joyce began to cry.

"Oh, don't cry." Harry edged his chair round next to hers and handed her a large white handkerchief.

He put an arm lightly round her shoulders until she gave a final gulp. "I'm so sorry," she whispered. "It's all been such a strain." She tried to hand him back his handkerchief, now liberally smeared with make-up. "Keep it," said Harry. Seeing she had recovered, he moved his chair back.

With bent head, she picked at her carrot cake and sipped a little tea.

"I'm sorry," she said again.

"Don't be," said Harry bracingly. "You've been through a terrible ordeal."

"It's worse. One of our sales reps has been found murdered."

"Really?"

"Isn't it in the paper?"

Harry silently cursed. He hadn't really been reading the paper. "I was looking for something else. Let me see. You're right! Here it is. Front page. Oh, you poor thing."

"I'm so frightened," said Joyce. "What if someone is out to murder the lot of us?"

"I shouldn't think so for a moment. Did Mr. Smedley have any enemies?"

"Everybody loved him," said Joyce and began to cry again.

He waited patiently until she had again recovered and said, "Look, you need something to take your mind off things. I bought two tickets for the production of *The Mikado* that's on tonight. But my girl-friend's just broken off with me. Would you like to come along? Cheer you up. No strings."

She gave him a watery smile. "I'd like that. I hate being in the house on my own."

"There you are then. That's all set. Let me get the bill. No, I insist." Harry called over the waitress and paid, extracting a note from a wallet stuffed with money. He left a generous tip on the table.

"I'll pick you up at seven."

"You don't know where I live. Or my name. I'm Joyce Wilson."

"And I'm James Henderson."

Harry leaned across the table. "Fact is, I feel I've known you for ages. What's the address?"

"More tea, Mr. Witherspoon?"

"Yes, please. Do call me Phil. I must say these sponge cakes of yours are as light as a feather."

"I like a man with a good appetite."

Phil had found a particularly flattering photograph of Mabel he had taken at the Ancombe sale of work. It showed Mabel behind the jam counter standing in a shaft of sunlight from the high window above her. The light had cast an aureole around her head. He had used that as an excuse to call on her.

He felt so relaxed and at ease that he did not want to talk about murder. Her sitting room was so pleasant and her baking superb. She was everything he thought a woman should be. He sometimes had to confess to himself that Agatha Raisin could be very intimidating.

But mindful of duty, he asked, "Have you any idea who could have murdered Burt?"

"I've been thinking and thinking about it. The only thing is those dreadful videos the police told me about. People who look at things like that on the Internet are sick and dangerous. I think one of his weird customers found out where he was and killed him in a rage."

"The police are interviewing all the men who checked into the Web site. Maybe they'll come up with something."

"Of course, I heard at one of the staff parties that he had a bit of a reputation as a philanderer. Maybe some jilted female."

"I thought he was deeply in love with Jessica."

"My dear Phil. If you really love someone you don't have them cavorting on some dirty Web site."

"I thought at first that Burt might have killed Jessica, but he had a cast-iron alibi."

"I really don't believe in cast-iron alibis. But let's talk about something else. Tell me about yourself."

After half an hour, Phil reddened and said apologetically, "You must forgive me. I usually don't talk about myself much. You are such a good listener."

"And you are such an interesting man. Do you like Gilbert and Sullivan?"

"Very much."

"I am on the board of the Mircester Operatic Society. They are putting on *The Mikado*. Would you like to see it?"

"Very much."

"If you call here for me at, say, six-thirty, I'll take you along. I always have tickets left for me at the box office."

Agatha and Charles had spent an exhausting day interviewing all the neighbours in Burt's street. She called all the staff into the office for five-thirty. She and Charles planned to go back out when Burt's immediate neighbours came home from work. She hoped the police had found out where the neighbours worked and had already interviewed them, or they would not appreciate her presence.

"How did you get on?" Agatha asked Phil.

Phil did not want to tell Agatha about his proposed visit to *The Mikado*. He felt Agatha was jealous of Mabel's reputation as a domestic paragon. He said he hadn't got much further except that Mabel seemed doubtful about Burt's alibi.

"Is she, now?" said Agatha. "Maybe we should look into that alibi ourselves. What about you, Harry?"

He told them how he had engineered the meeting with Joyce and how he was taking her to see *The Mikado*. Phil was horrified. He could not now tell Agatha he was going himself. He cursed himself. After all, the whole point of his visit to Mabel was to get friendly with her. Now it was too late. Agatha would wonder why he had held that bit of information back. He'd need to have a private word with Harry.

"See you all here at nine in the morning," said Agatha.

"I won't be in," said Patrick. "I got the names of the men who checked into that Web site. Better you don't know how. I'm going to try to see some of them tonight, so it'll be a late evening for me. I might be a bit late in the morning."

"Fine," said Agatha.

Harry left quickly, and, with surprising agility, Phil raced after him down the stairs. "Wait, Harry," he said. "You can't go to *The Mikado*."

"Why?"

"Mabel's taking me there and she knows what you look like and of course she knows Joyce."

"Why didn't you say something upstairs?"

"Don't know," mumbled Phil.

"Damn, I'll think of somewhere else to take her."

Nine

Harry rang Joyce's doorbell. She appeared dressed in a cashmere stole under which she wore a little black dress, sheer stockings and very high heels. She appeared to have drenched herself in an overpowerful and very cheap scent.

Harry complimented her on her appearance while helping her into his car and all the time thinking she had such a rabbity face.

"I hope you won't be too disappointed," said Harry. "But *The Mikado* is off."

"Oh, why?"

"Well, I like the traditional stuff and someone told me this production is set in a modern-day factory with the whole chorus dressed in denim overalls. So what I thought instead is the Classic Cinema. They're showing *Brief Encounter.* Did you ever see it?"

"No."

"I thought we'd go there and then have dinner at the Royal afterwards."

Joyce's protuberant eyes widened. The

Royal was Mircester's best hotel and the restaurant was very expensive. She had tried several times to get Robert Smedley to take her there, but he'd always refused.

"Sounds lovely," she said.

Harry had taken the precaution of bringing two large handkerchiefs with him. Joyce cried her way through the whole black-and-white film.

"You must think me very silly," she said outside the cinema, "but it brought back a lot of sad memories."

"You mean you were in love with a married man?" asked Harry lightly.

"Oh, no, nothing like that. When we get to the hotel, I'll just go to the ladies' and repair my make-up."

So she wasn't going to admit to having an affair with Smedley, thought Harry.

Joyce came back. She picked up the large menu. "I always like fish," she said. She ordered avocado stuffed with prawns to start and then a whole grilled lobster. Harry had a feeling she was choosing by price rather than taste. Perhaps Smedley's attraction for her had been nothing more than money. He ordered pâté followed by boeuf bourguignon and also a half bottle of red wine for himself and a half bottle of white for Joyce.

She said coyly that she always liked to have a dry martini before eating. "Could you make it a large one?" she asked. "I'm quite nervous."

Harry expected the meal to be a fairly silent one. Joyce obviously did not want to talk about Smedley and he wanted to tell as few lies about his background as possible, but Joyce turned out to be loquacious enough for both of them. She prattled on about her parents, father now dead and her mother in care in Bath. She talked about a previous job as secretary to a supermarket manager — "I didn't even get a discount on my groceries" — and Harry tried not to let his eyes glaze over with boredom.

He kept trying to turn the conversation back to the murder and Joyce always kept on talking about something else.

She finished her meal with crêpes Suzette, then brandy and coffee. Harry paid the bill with cash. He did not want to use a credit card in case Joyce could read the name on it, which wasn't the one he'd given her.

When he drove her home, she asked him if he would like to come in for a coffee. Harry reluctantly agreed.

Perhaps he might have a chance for a quick search.

"Now just relax," said Joyce, "and I'll put the kettle on. Be back in a tick."

Harry moved quietly about the room, searching here, searching there, seeing if there was anything that might provide some lead on the case.

Phil had enjoyed his evening immensely. At times he felt guilty that he had not found out anything at all but consoled himself with the thought that such a fine woman as Mabel had nothing to hide.

By the time she had invited him home for coffee they were talking like old friends, and it was with great reluctance that he finally got up to leave. Suddenly as shy as a schoolboy, he hesitated in the doorway. "I've enjoyed myself so much. I'd like to do this again."

Mabel smiled. "What about Saturday? We could take a drive in the country and have a picnic."

"I would love that."

"Let's make a day of it. Pick me up about ten in the morning."

"Wonderful."

Meanwhile, Harry realized that the seconds were ticking into minutes and still Joyce hadn't appeared.

"Joyce!" he called.

"Here," she said huskily.

He swung round. Joyce was standing in the doorway wearing nothing but a transparent black nightie. She held out her hand. "Let's forget about the coffee."

Oh, Agatha Raisin, mourned Harry inwardly. The things I do for you!

He allowed himself to be led upstairs to the bedroom. Joyce was staggering slightly, all she had drunk evidently just having begun to hit her.

"Where's the bathroom?" asked Harry, stalling for time. "I need a shower."

"Just out of the door and turn right. I'll be waiting."

Harry went into the bathroom and locked the door. He ran a bath instead. He undressed and tried to relax in the warm water. He wished he were one of those fellows who could get excited at the prospect of sex with any woman.

He soaked as long as he could and then got out and dried himself. He picked up his clothes and went into the bedroom.

Joyce was fast asleep and snoring lustily. With a sigh of relief, he quietly got into his clothes.

He was about to make a smart exit. Then he noticed a bureau against the wall farthest away from the bed.

He tiptoed over and softly began to pull out the drawers. He didn't expect to find any letters because nobody, surely, wrote letters in these days of email and text messages.

There were bank statements and credit card receipts. He was about to give up when he saw an envelope tucked at the back of the bottom drawer. He drew it out. Joyce had left lamps burning on either side of the bed.

The envelope was addressed to Joyce and in the top corner was written, "By Hand."

He slid out the letter. Bingo! The letter, which he quickly scanned, was from Burt Haviland. He shoved it in his pocket.

Harry went down the stairs and softly let himself out of the front door. He had lied to Joyce about living with his parents. As a precaution, he had even lied about where they lived. He had a little flat in the centre of Mircester.

As soon as he was home, he sat down and read the letter carefully. Burt had written: "Dear Joyce, I can't go on seeing you because Smedley is my boss and if he finds out we've been having an affair, I'll lose my job and you'll lose your house.

Thanks for everything, pet, but let's just let the whole thing drop. Love, Burt."

Harry whistled under his breath. "I wonder what Agatha will make of this."

Phil arrived before Harry next morning. "I went out with Mabel last night," said Phil, deciding that withholding information from Agatha could be dangerous. "How did you get on?" asked Agatha.

"I didn't find out anything," said Phil. "You see, in my opinion, Mabel Smedley is a thoroughly nice woman. What you see is what you get. But we've become friends and I'm taking her out on Saturday. She might let something slip if there's anything to let slip."

"Keep after it." Agatha regarded Phil narrowly. He was looking happy and much younger than his years. "Don't fancy her, do you?" she asked.

Phil coloured. "Don't be ridiculous. A man of my age!"

"Okay. Here's Harry."

She listened excitedly as Harry told her about the attempted seduction and finding the letter. Then she said, "Now, why didn't the police find it? They must have searched her house."

"Maybe they missed it."

"I doubt it. Maybe she put it somewhere and put it back after the police had left. Although, why someone would want to keep a Dear John — or, in her case, Dear Jane — letter is beyond me. I'd better tell the police. Damn! It's not like the old days. I don't want to get on the wrong side of them. I want Bill Wong because he might trade some information. I'm not going to talk to anyone else. I'll go to police headquarters. You come with me, Harry. I'll phone Patrick and get him to liaise with you, Phil. Unless he's got a hot lead on any of the men who accessed that Web site, I want you to get to some of Smedley's staff and find out who else Haviland was romancing."

She telephoned Patrick and gave him instructions and then said to Phil, "He'll meet you in the square in fifteen minutes."

Agatha was told Bill Wong was out on a case. She and Harry waited in reception.

While they waited, a policeman and policewoman came out, putting on their helmets. "Where are you off to?" asked the desk sergeant.

"Folks up in Bewdley Road are complaining some hysterical woman's been harassing them. Honestly, if it weren't a posh area, we wouldn't have to bother."

When they had left, Harry whispered, "Could you step outside for a moment?"

Agatha followed him out.

"What?"

"I told Joyce my name was James Henderson and I lived with my parents on Bewdley Road. They actually live in a cottage out in the country. She's a greedy thing and must be frantic at the idea of a rich young man slipping through her fingers. I bet it's her."

"Serves her right."

"Where's Charles?"

"Decided to sleep late. Oh, here's Bill. Bill, we must talk to you urgently. We've got important information."

He walked them through to the interview room and listened intently while Agatha told him about the letter. Then he read it.

Bill leaned back in his chair. "Agatha, have you thought for a moment what Wilkes will say when he finds out how you went about getting this letter? Young Harry here lying about his name and job and then stealing it while she was asleep? He'll come down on you like a ton of bricks."

"Couldn't you just say we found it and

cannot reveal our sources?"

"You're not a journalist."

"Say it was delivered to our office anonymously this morning," said Harry.

"Come on, Bill," urged Agatha. "It's too important a piece of information to hold back. If you tell the truth and get us into trouble, what'll happen to Harry?"

"I know," said Harry. "There's nothing wrong with part of the truth. Say Joyce picked me up in a tea shop. I made a date with her because she didn't know who I worked for and I thought I might get some information by taking her out for dinner. She drank too much. I took her home. She invited me in for coffee, went to make it and disappeared. I went to look for her and found her dead asleep in the bedroom. I searched her bureau because that's my job and found the letter."

"So far, so good. But he'll be furious at you for taking the letter away."

"If you give me an hour, I'll put it back," said Harry.

"How?"

"I'll find a way. Please."

"I should be shot for agreeing to this. Okay. But if you're caught, I know nothing about it."

"Thanks." Harry took the letter and left.

"Now Bill," said Agatha. "What about giving me some crumbs of information?"

"As long as you don't say you got it from me."

"Of course."

"Burt Haviland's bank account reveals that in the past six months he received two payments of twenty thousand pounds each."

"Blackmail?"

"Could be. It was paid in cash. The teller who took the payments has left the bank and is now on holiday in Turkey. We're trying to find her."

"I keep wondering if all these murders aren't connected in some way," said Agatha.

"Maybe. You'd better get off. I'll tell everyone it was just a friendly call. Oh, by the way, my parents are still thrilled with that lamp."

"Good."

"They only wish they could afford the other one."

"What other one?"

"There's a blue one in the shop now and Mum thinks it would be a companion to the other. I'd buy it, but I'm overdrawn at the bank as it is."

Agatha repressed a sigh. "I'll get it for them."

"No, it's too much. Don't even think of it."

It was only when Agatha had paid for the other lamp and sent it off in a taxi that she reflected that Mr. Wong ran a very successful dry-cleaning business and could easily have afforded it. But she got a warm feeling just thinking how pleased Bill would be.

Harry went to his flat first. Wearing a pair of thin latex gloves, he took out an envelope similar to the one containing the letter and copied out a forgery of the "By Hand" legend. The police did not have his fingerprints but they might have Agatha's. Of course they also might wonder why there were no fingerprints on the envelope at all, but that was a minor problem. Then he realized that his fingerprints and Agatha's would be all over the letter itself. He would need to replace it with a copy. He ran off a copy on his printer. Then he dressed himself in a pair of worker's overalls he had once used when he was painting his flat. He padded out his cheeks, dug into a box of costumes he had worn when he was in the school dramatic society and found a heavy fake moustache, which he glued on with spirit gum. Putting on a pair of dark sunglasses and pulling a baseball cap down low on his head, he went out and stopped off at a hardware shop to buy a toolbox. He set off on his motorbike and left it at the end of Joyce's street.

He walked boldly up to Joyce's front door and rang the bell. She opened the door. He felt a guilty pang when he saw her eyes were red with weeping.

"What is it?"

Joyce lived in a terraced house. Harry flashed his student rail card so quickly that no one could possibly have seen it clearly and said, "I'm from the council. Your neighbours are worried about subsidence. Just going to check the walls."

"Come in. Don't be long. I've got to go out."

Harry made a great show of tapping the walls. The trouble was Joyce followed his every move. He was just wondering how he could ever put that letter back without her noticing when there was a ring at the doorbell.

Harry heard a stern voice. "Detective Inspector Wilkes. We have a warrant to search these premises."

Harry heard Joyce complain. "I'm not letting you in. You've already searched them."

"If you do not let us in, we will need to

take you down to the station."

Harry ran lightly up the stairs. He slipped the letter back into the drawer, opened the bedroom window, threw his toolbox into the back garden, stepped out and, hanging on to the drainpipe, closed the window and slithered down. Thanking his stars that the back of Joyce's house was not overlooked by any other houses and was a jungle of untended trees and bushes which shielded him from Joyce's neighbours on either side, he made his way out by the back garden gate, along a lane and out into the main road.

How had Wilkes been able to move so quickly?

The fact was that Bill had told Wilkes almost immediately he had heard a rumour that Joyce had been having an affair with Haviland and that evidence of that may have been overlooked during the initial search. Although he had expected it would take some time to get a search warrant, Wilkes had pointed out that the original search warrant was still legal, called together a search team, and set out.

Bill hoped that Harry, who he believed was probably out on the street, watching the house and waiting for Joyce to leave, would not be discovered.

Joyce tried to follow the search team upstairs, but Wilkes had brought along a policewoman who ushered Joyce into her living room and told her to sit down and wait.

They came to the bureau. One said, "It's just all bank statements and accounts. I've been through this before."

"Look again," snapped Wilkes.

The detective pulled open the bottom drawer. Harry had simply dropped the letter right on the top.

He took the envelope and extracted the letter and read it. "Take a look at this, sir," he said, handing it to Wilkes.

Wilkes read it. "Odd. It looks like a copy. Let's go downstairs and see what our Miss Wilson has to say for herself."

Joyce, confronted by the letter, burst into floods of tears. The policewoman handed her a box of tissues which was lying on the coffee table, and then all waited in stolid silence until she had stopped crying.

"It was just a brief fling," she said.

"I think you had better accompany us to the police station."

"What about the building inspector?"

"What building inspector?"

"He was here when you arrived."

They searched the house and then came back to Joyce. "No sign of anyone. Why was he here?"

"He said there was subsidence next door and needed to check the walls."

"Did he show you any identification?"

"He flashed some sort of card."

"Probably some burglar trying it on who fled when we arrived," said Wilkes. "We'll check with the neighbours and then, Miss Wilson, you're coming to the station with us."

As Joyce was led into police headquarters, a policeman in reception turned and stared at her and then hurried after Wilkes. "Sir?" he called.

"Take her to interview room number two," said Wilkes. "Yes, Phelps, what is it?"

"That woman you've just brought in. She answers the description of a woman who was up at Bewdley Road early this morning, harassing the residents and demanding to see someone called James Henderson."

"Thanks, Phelps, we'll ask her about that."

It was obvious to Wilkes that his first

question genuinely amazed Joyce. "Did Mr. Robert Smedley tell you he was being blackmailed?"

"No! And he would have done. He told me everything."

"So tell us about Burt Haviland. Did you know he was originally called Bert Smellie and did a term in prison for armed robbery?"

Those protuberant eyes of hers looked ready to pop out of their sockets. "I can't believe that. He was a good salesman. He loved me."

"How could he love you when he knew you were having an affair with the boss?"

"I am fascinating to men," said Joyce. She was regaining her composure. I wonder whether she can cry at will, thought Wilkes. I wonder if this one is more devious than we ever imagined.

"This letter is a copy. Where's the original?"

Joyce looked genuinely surprised. "I don't know."

With a few breaks, the questioning went on all day. Joyce became calmer and calmer as the day went on. She stuck to her story that she had had a brief affair with Burt only because she didn't think Smedley meant to marry her. But shortly after Burt broke up with her, Smedley had said that he would start proceedings for a divorce within the month.

The only time she seemed to lose some of her composure was when Wilkes asked her what she was doing out at Bewdley Road where the residents had described her as hysterical.

"Someone called James Henderson took me out last night. He picked me up. I think he put that date rape drug in my drink because when I woke up this morning, he was gone. I was furious. He said he lived with his parents out on Bewdley Road. I went to confront him. He must have taken the letter and copied it."

"Were you raped?"

"No, he must have got cold feet."

"We'll have you tested for drugs."

"That won't be necessary."

"Miss Wilson, you tell us that someone calling himself James Henderson slipped you a Mickey and yet you don't want a test?"

"I may have been mistaken," said Joyce sulkily. She knew now she'd gone frantic at the thought of such a rich prize slipping through her fingers.

After Agatha had put Harry back on two outstanding divorce cases and she had spent most of the day making notes on the murders without coming to any conclusion, Charles put in an appearance. They decided to go and confront Mabel Smedley. Agatha thought it would be better to leave Phil behind, and let Mabel go on thinking that Phil was a friend.

Agatha started the questioning, "Mrs. Smedley . . ."

"Mabel, please."

"Well, Mabel, you must know by now that Joyce Wilson was really having an affair with your husband."

"So the police keep trying to tell me. I still don't believe it. He was merely kind to her, taking her to Bath to see her mother. He told me all about it, you know."

"Did you know that the police have proof that Joyce was also having an affair with Burt Haviland?"

"That's possible. Burt had a bit of a reputation. He probably killed that Jessica girl and someone killed him in revenge."

"I see your house is up for sale," said Charles. "I noticed the estate agent's board on the way in."

"Yes, I've decided to make a clean start. The factory has been sold to another electronics company. It will be up to them if they want to retain the staff."

"When is your husband's funeral?"

"Let me see, last Friday."

"There was nothing in the papers about it."

"I suppose it's old news. The police released his body. I had him cremated. That's him over there." She pointed at the sideboard. A black urn sat on top of it. "I like to have him with me. I talk to him sometimes. But all this chit-chat is surely not helping you find my husband's murderer."

"I'm beginning to think it might have been Joyce Wilson," said Agatha.

"Joyce is a simpleton. Not a bad secretary as secretaries go, but pretty dim."

"It doesn't take much intelligence to put weedkiller in a milk bottle."

"It takes a lot of nerve to stand up under the strain of a murder inquiry. Believe me, if Joyce had done it, she would have burst into tears by now and confessed all."

"The poor woman's under a lot of strain herself," said Charles as they drove off.

"She was as cool as cucumbers."

"I thought from her body language she was quite rigid. No more cosy cups of coffee either."

"I'm beginning to think this all leads

somehow to Jessica."

"Could be coincidence. Jessica could just have been in the wrong place at the wrong time."

"Then you would think it would've been a sex crime. It was made to look like one. An amateur murderer."

"Or one just playing for time."

Agatha squinted at her watch. "It's after six. We couldn't get near Burt's neighbours last night because the police were all over the place. Let's try again."

But they found there was a mobile police unit set up in the street and policemen were still busy making door-to-door enquiries.

"There's a pub two streets back," said Charles. "Go back there. We might find some of the locals talking about the murder."

The pub was called The Prince of Wales. No brewery had got around to modernizing it. It was dingy with cigarette burns on the green linoleum on the floor. There was a pool table at one end and a row of machines — video computer games and one-arm bandits — at the other.

The pub was quite busy. "Where do we start?" asked Agatha.

"At the bar. Your usual?"

"No, just tonic water."

Charles ordered a tonic water for Agatha and a Coke for himself. "What are all the police doing around here?" he asked the barman.

"Haven't you heard? Chap was murdered. Stabbed to death."

"How awful," said Agatha. "Does anyone know who did it?"

"Not as far as I know. You could ask Mr. Burden, the chap with the cap over in the corner. He said the police asked him so many questions, he began to feel he'd done it himself."

"He's a neighbour?"

"Next-door flat."

Mr. Burden was sitting alone at a small round table. He was a small neat man in a dark business suit, collar and tie, and with a tweed cap on his head.

"Mr. Burden?" asked Agatha.

"Yes, who wants to know?"

Charles and Agatha sat down next to him. "We're private detectives working on this murder of Burt Haviland. Did you hear anything?"

"What's that you're drinking?" asked Charles.

An empty half-pint glass was in front of

Mr. Burden. He brightened visibly. "Very kind of you. I'll have a double Scotch."

Charles looked hopefully at Agatha, who refused to meet his gaze. Let him pay for something for once, she thought.

They waited until Charles had returned.

"Now," said Agatha. "Did you hear anything?"

"I heard him screaming. I know now it must have been him, but at the time I thought it was the telly. Then I heard the door slam and footsteps running down the stairs."

"The police said no one was at home except a deaf old lady on the top floor."

"I was off sick. First time they came round and I heard them hammering, I didn't answer. I was feeling poorly and I was in bed. Food poisoning."

Agatha looked at the glass Mr. Burden had just drained, wondering whether alcohol poisoning would be nearer the mark.

"What kind of footsteps?" she asked.

He twisted his empty glass this way and that.

"I'm sure Mr. Burden would like another one, Charles," said Agatha hurriedly.

Charles sighed and went back to the bar.

When he returned, Mr. Burden seized the glass eagerly and took a swig of whisky.

"Footsteps," prompted Agatha.

"What do you mean?"

"Were they heavy, light, heels, what?"

He frowned. "Quick, light, sort of click, clack, click clack."

"Like high heels?"

"That's it."

Charles and Agatha exchanged glances. They were looking for a woman.

Ten

Agatha and Charles sat in Agatha's cottage that evening going over every little bit of the three murder cases they could think of.

"It's this business about a woman," said Charles. "We've got Joyce and we've got Mabel."

"And neither of them with any link to Jessica," Agatha pointed out.

"Oh, yes, there is. Jessica was in love with Burt. Burt worked for Smedleys Electronics. Burt had an affair with Joyce."

"I'm tired," complained Agatha. "I'm not thinking clearly. Let's walk along to the pub and have something to eat."

When they opened the door, it was to find the rain was lashing down. "Why on earth did I get an air conditioner?" moaned Agatha. "We'll walk anyway. I feel like having a good stiff drink." Charles took a large umbrella from beside the door and, huddled under its shelter, they walked briskly to the pub.

The Red Lion was an old Georgian pub

with steps down into the bar. Agatha went down the first step, winced as a pain shot through her hip, and clutched Charles's arm.

"What's up?" he asked.

"Nothing," lied Agatha. "Just wrenched my ankle a little."

Agatha was greeted by various locals. One of them said, "Evening, Mrs. Raisin. Nice to see you and your young man."

Agatha felt immediately depressed. She was in her early fifties and Charles was in his forties. Was the age difference so evident? Maybe she wouldn't live long. She was getting old. Charles's voice drifted away as she began to plan her own funeral. James Lacey would come back for it. He would cry and say, "I've lost the best woman I've ever known." A tear rolled down Agatha's cheek.

"Hey!" exclaimed Charles. "You're crying."

Agatha brushed the tear away. "Just tired," she said defensively.

"Maybe you should give up this detective business. It was easier for you when you were an amateur."

"Oh, I'll survive. What are we having to eat?"

"We can have scampi and chips, lasagne

and chips, curried chicken and chips or the all-day breakfast," said Charles, reading the items off a blackboard on the other side of the bar. "I think the all-day breakfast would be safest."

"Okay."

Charles ordered two. A table by the open fire had just been vacated and they took their drinks over to it.

"Let's think," said Charles. "Did you hear a word I said while we were waiting for the drinks?"

"Not really."

"I was talking about Phil and Harry. Phil is spending the day with Mabel on Saturday. We'll need to impress on him that as nice as Mabel seems, he's really got to keep his eyes and ears open. Then what about Harry and Joyce?"

"Speak of the devil," said Agatha, looking across the bar. Harry had just entered the pub. "He looks almost human."

Harry's hair had grown a little. He was still minus studs and earrings, and he was wearing the outfit he had worn when he had picked up Joyce in the tea shop. Agatha waved him over. He pulled out a chair and sat down.

"What brings you here?" asked Charles. "Any news?"

"No, I came to ask you that."

"I should have phoned you," said Agatha. "Did you get the letter back?"

"Just." Harry told them about the sudden arrival of the police. "I'll get myself a drink. What about you two?"

"We're all right at the moment," said Charles. "Just waiting for food."

Harry went to the bar and came back with a half pint of beer.

"What do you feel about romancing Joyce again?" asked Agatha.

"Can't. She knows me as James Henderson, who told her he lived with his parents on the Bewdley Road. She'd be very suspicious if I put in an appearance again and she might tell the police. Then there's that letter. I was stupid to take it away. The detective agency might be the first place they think of when they're wondering who took a copy."

"Did the police ever search Mabel's house?" asked Charles.

"I don't think they did a thorough forensic search," said Agatha. "I think she just let them go through all his papers and search his home computer."

Harry said, "Don't tell me you suspect that lady of all the virtues?"

Charles told him about Mr. Burden

hearing what sounded like someone in high heels fleeing the scene of the murder.

"Have you ever seen Mabel Smedley in anything other than flat shoes?" asked Harry. "Doesn't even wear make-up."

"Phil is spending the day with her to-morrow. We're going to ask him to try to get a proper look around. And did we tell you that Smedley may have been black-mailed? Or someone else? Two deposits of twenty thousand pounds were paid into Haviland's account — cash."

"The way I see it . . ." said Harry. "Oh, here's your food."

"Don't you want anything?" asked Charles.

"Nothing like that. I'll eat later. I was about to say that if Smedley was black-mailed and as his home computer had been overwritten, he might have been watching the girls' Web site."

"But if it was Smedley who paid the money," said Charles, "the withdrawals would show on his bank account."

"Unless, of course, the money came out of the firm," said Harry, "and Joyce fiddled the books to cover it up. But I'm forgetting there is no record of Smedley having checked into that Web site."

"There must be something," protested

Agatha, "or he wouldn't have overwritten what was on his computer. Now, there's a thing. As far as I can gather, everything on his home computer was overwritten right up until his death."

"Meaning Mabel might have done it, even though she claims not to know one end of a computer from the other."

Agatha's mobile rang and she took it out of her handbag. It was Bill. "Agatha, I'm sending you a cheque for that other lamp. I didn't mean you to buy it. It's too much."

"Nonsense. I hope your parents are pleased."

"Pleased! They're thrilled to bits. Mum wants you and Charles to come over for dinner on Sunday."

"Oh, how lovely. But we're both working flat out. When all these murders are solved, we'll make a party of it. Please don't bother sending me a cheque. I'd just tear it up. What is Joyce saying?"

"Stonewalling at every turn, or rather that's the way it seems to Wilkes. Do you know, Harry may have slipped up a little with that letter. There were no fingerprints on the envelope. And the letter was a copy. Where's the original?"

"I'll see him about that," said Agatha.

When she rang off, she asked Harry,

"Why *did* you replace the letter with a copy?"

"Because my fingerprints and yours would have been all over the original."

"It may make the police begin to wonder more about Joyce's mysterious Mr. Henderson and they may begin to look in your direction. Also, you'd better go back to the Gothic look or whatever that was you were adopting when I first met you. I mean, if you should run into Joyce by accident, you might just be able to sneer your way out of it and look as far from the rich young James Henderson as possible. Better lie low for a bit and get on with the divorce cases."

"I'm nearly finished with those. Phil lent me an excellent camera. I'll have all the stuff for you tomorrow."

"I think when we eat this," said Agatha, "we should all go and visit Phil. I think he admires Mabel too much. We need to stiffen his spine."

Agatha noticed that Phil did not look particularly pleased to see them. "Have we interrupted anything?" she asked.

"I was just watching television."

He led the way into his living room. Agatha noticed the television set was switched off.

"Sit down. What can I do for you?"

Agatha told him about Mr. Burden hearing a woman's footsteps. "So," she finished, "we're looking for a woman and the two women we have are Mabel and Joyce."

"And Trixie and Fairy. And whoever else Burt Haviland might have been having an affair with," said Phil.

"You don't want it to be Mabel, do you?" asked Charles.

Phil looked flustered. "My feelings don't enter into this, but my common sense does. It is my reasoned opinion that Mabel Smedley would not hurt a fly."

"I think it might be possible," said Agatha. "Look, Phil, the reason we called is to urge you to keep an open mind. When you're in her house, keep looking around discreetly."

"And what am I supposed to be looking for?" asked Phil bitterly. "A recipe for angel cakes?"

"Phil, please," urged Charles. "Just do your job."

"Of course I will keep an eye out for anything suspicious," said Phil. "Now, if you don't mind, I have some work in the darkroom to do."

"I think he's smitten with her," said Agatha as they walked to her cottage

227

through the rain. "Snakes and bastards!" The nasty weather was making her edgy, but she hoped it would continue to rain on Saturday. It might take a bit of the gloss off the crush she was sure Phil had on Mabel.

But the English weather made one of its mercurial changes by Friday evening and Saturday dawned sunny, warm and cloudless.

Phil set out for Mabel's home, trying to put what Agatha had said to the back of his mind because he did not want his day to be spoiled. He felt a sharp pang of disappointment when he saw the "For Sale" sign.

Mabel answered the door to him wearing a flowery dress with a Peter Pan collar and a drooping hemline. Phil thought she looked every inch the lady she obviously was.

"I didn't know you were selling up," said Phil. "Not leaving the area, I hope?"

"No, I plan to find somewhere nearby but much smaller."

"Where would you like to go today?" asked Phil.

"There's a nice glade with a stream running through it on Lord Pendlebury's estate."

Lord Pendlebury was a local landowner

well known for his dislike of ramblers and other trespassers.

"I'm afraid we won't be allowed anywhere on that estate," said Phil.

"It's all right. I phoned him and asked for his permission."

Phil was impressed.

She had a picnic basket ready, which he loaded into the boot of his car. There was a bit of the old-fashioned village snob about Phil and he privately thought that anyone who was a friend of Lord Pendlebury's must be all right.

With Mabel directing him, they drove back to Carsely and then up the hill leading out of the village.

They left the car outside a gate at the back of the estate and Phil, carrying rugs and picnic basket, followed Mabel through the trees.

She stopped in a little grassy glade. A silver stream wound its way through the glade and the sun filtered down through the green leaves above.

Phil spread the rugs on the grass while Mabel opened the hamper. She had prepared a simple lunch of cold chicken and salad, with a bottle of white wine and slabs of rich fruitcake and a thermos of coffee to follow.

They talked about books they had read and places they had seen. Philip had never felt so at ease with a woman in his whole life.

Then suddenly she asked him how Agatha was getting on solving the murder cases.

"Not very far," said Phil. "But she seems to think all the murders are tied up in some way and that they were done by a woman."

"More coffee?"

"Please."

"Why a woman?"

Phil told her about Mr. Burden hearing footsteps that sounded like a woman wearing heels.

Mabel smiled. "That lets me out. I *never* wear heels."

"Oh, Mabel," said Phil with a rush of affection. "No one could possibly suspect a lady like you."

"Shall we be getting back?" asked Mabel. "Where has the afternoon gone?"

Phil fretted as he drove her home, wondering how to prolong the day, trying to find the courage to ask her out for dinner.

At her house, she invited him in. "Would you like a drink?" she asked. "I know you're driving, but one won't harm you."

"I'm a beer drinker."

"I have a cold beer in the fridge."

She went off to the kitchen. Phil glanced around the living room. The hell with looking for clues, he thought. Waste of time.

He studied his face in the mirror over the fireplace, wondering if he looked too old. He was just about to turn away when his eye fell on a stiff folded piece of paper on the mantelpiece. He would take a quick look at it to justify his work at the detective agency, and that was all he was going to do. He opened it. It was a diploma from Mircester College, made out to Mabel Smedley for completing a computer course. He heard her coming and quickly replaced it.

She had said she knew nothing about computers.

He forced himself to sit and drink the beer and talk a little longer. All thoughts of extending the visit had gone out of his head. He simply wanted to get away and mull over what he had seen. There must be an innocent explanation.

Bill Wong had been summoned by Detective Inspector Wilkes despite the fact that it was his day off. He reluctantly left his gardening and made his way to police headquarters.

"I'll get right to the point," said Wilkes. "You're friendly with that Raisin woman, right?"

"Yes, sir."

"In my opinion she's a blundering amateur who employs blundering amateurs. That young man who works for her. What's his name?"

"Harry Beam."

"I think he may be our mysterious Mr. Henderson. Now Joyce says this Henderson picked her up in the Abbey Tea Rooms and then took her to dinner at the Royal. Check both places and get a description. If it is Harry Beam, we'll get him in here for questioning."

"Now, sir?"

"Yes. Now."

Bill phoned Agatha and told her to get hold of Harry Beam and to meet him at her office.

"What's it all about?" asked Agatha half an hour later as she, Charles and Harry were confronted by Bill.

"It's like this. Wilkes is pretty sure Harry here is the mysterious James Henderson. I'm supposed to be checking those places you took her for a description."

Harry was back in his leather gear, earrings and studs. "It's all right. I didn't look like this." Harry gave Bill a description of what he was wearing.

"Good," said Bill. "That should get us all out of this. Agatha, never again drag me into your schemes. I like to do everything by the book. What if Joyce is the murderess? What if she did kill Haviland? We can't produce a copy of a letter in court, even though she does admit it's a copy of the original. She could change her tune. Say she lied because of brutal police questioning. All right, I'll give it an hour and then go back and tell Wilkes that Henderson bears no resemblance to Harry here. Now, to soothe my ruffled feelings, have you found out anything that might be of use?"

Agatha shook her head. At that moment her mobile rang. She answered it and listened and gave a sharp exclamation. Then she said, "I'm at the office with Harry, Charles and Bill Wong. You'd better come here."

"What was that all about?" asked Bill when she rang off.

"Phil found a diploma in Mabel's house — a diploma for computer studies."

They discussed the possible significance of this until Phil arrived.

"Good work," said Bill. "We'll need to pull her in again for questioning. She swore blind she knew nothing about computers."

Phil looked distressed. "She'll guess it was me."

"Does that matter?" asked Agatha.

Phil did not want to believe Mabel guilty of anything. "Couldn't you just check with the college? They'll have records. I mean, if you destroy my friendship with her, I won't be able to find out anything else."

"Good point," said Agatha. "When are you seeing her again?"

"I was so flustered, I didn't make another date."

"Better do it as soon as possible."

Bill looked cross. "Who's running this investigation? You or the police?"

"Both of us," said Agatha soothingly.

"If the facts of that letter come out, I could be suspended from duty and maybe even lose my job. Don't ever embroil me in one of your mad amateur schemes again."

"We're not amateurs," said Agatha huffily.

"Could've fooled me. I'll be off to Mircester College," said Bill. "Hope there

234

is someone there on a Saturday evening. I'll tell Wilkes I had a brainwave."

"You might at least thank us," said Agatha.

Bill paused in the doorway. "Agatha, wasn't life *safer* in public relations?"

Agatha grinned. "Dog-eat-dog, I assure you. Knives in backs all round."

"And stale metaphors by the dozen," murmured Charles as Bill left, slamming the door behind him.

Her mobile rang again. Agatha listened and said, "We're all in the office. You'd better come in until we figure out what to do about this."

She rang off and said, "Patrick's found out something about that maths teacher."

Patrick arrived half an hour later. He looked weary. He sank down on the sofa and said, "Could someone make me a cup of coffee? I'm beat."

"I'll do it," said Harry. "Detective work wearing you out?"

"No, it's my home life. We'd both agreed on a divorce, but she wants me out of the house now. I sold my flat when we got married. Prices have gone sky-high, so I don't know if I can afford to buy anything, and rents are pretty steep as well."

"You can move in with me until you find a place," said Phil. "I've got a spare room."

"Phil's very neat," cautioned Agatha. "You're not messy, are you, Patrick?"

"Not in the slightest. That's what her indoors was always complaining about. She said I tidied things away so much, she couldn't find anything."

Agatha cynically reflected that Miss Simms — as she always thought of her — had probably found a new gentleman friend and wanted rid of Patrick as soon as possible.

"Thanks a lot, Phil," said Patrick. "We'll get together later and agree on the rent."

Harry handed Patrick a cup of instant coffee.

"Now," said Agatha impatiently, "what's this about that maths teacher? Charles, what are you looking at?"

Charles was staring down from the window. "I've just seen Laura Ward-Barkinson. Back in a minute."

He rushed off.

Agatha felt a pang on jealousy and then reminded herself firmly that Charles was only a friend. In any case, this Laura might simply be a friend of his aunt.

"So what's it about, Patrick?" Agatha

moved to the window and looked down. Charles was talking animatedly to a tall, leggy brunette. Then they moved off together.

"I don't think you're listening," said Patrick sharply.

"Sorry." Agatha moved away from the window.

"I was saying that Owen, the maths teacher, was seen one evening several weeks before Jessica was murdered out at the Pheasant restaurant on the road to Pershore. It's very posh, but I know the owner from the days when I was in the force. I met him by chance in Evesham when I was getting my hair cut — what's left of it. We went for a drink and I began discussing the case. Funnily enough, I'd quite forgotten I'd once asked Phil to wait outside the school and take a photo of Owen Trump, that teacher. He was in the notes, Agatha, but no picture. Anyway, my friend, John Wheeler, he said to me he might look at photos because he knew so many people in the area and he might recognize someone. I had a whole set of prints in my briefcase and he went through them. He picked out Owen Trump. He remembered him because he'd made such a fuss about the wine and then complained about the food. He hadn't recognized Jessica first time round, so I showed him a photograph of her again. He said she'd had her hair up and was wearing a lot of make-up and looked much older. He said she seemed embarrassed by Owen's behaviour and was drinking rather a lot."

"Let's look up the phone book and find out where he lives," said Agatha.

"Already got his address." Patrick produced a thick notebook. "He's got a flat in the centre of Mircester."

"All right. Patrick and I will go. Phil, you may as well see if you can make another date with Mabel. Harry, I think you should keep out of sight for the moment. Oh, if Charles comes back, tell him about this latest development."

After they had left, Harry paced up and down the office, coming to a halt before the mirror behind Mrs. Freedman's desk. He suddenly thought he looked ridiculous. Why had he ever thought all this piercing and leather cool? He decided to go home and change, make up some sort of disguise and follow Joyce. In Harry's mind, all roads led to Joyce. She had had affairs with both Burt and Smedley. She had served the lethal coffee. If he followed her, she might betray herself in some way.

***

Owen Trump was at home. He gave them a supercilious glare when he saw who was standing outside his door.

"We want to ask you a few questions," said Agatha.

"If there are any questions to answer, I will speak to the police. Now, go away."

"All right," said Agatha. "We'll go straight to the police now and tell them about your dinner with Jessica Bradley at the Pheasant."

He had half closed the door. He opened it wide again and said, "You'd better come in."

I can practically see the wheels turning in his brain, thought Agatha. The living room reeked of stale cigarette smoke and there were empty beer cans on the coffee table.

"It's like this," began Owen. "Oh, do sit down."

Agatha and Patrick sat down on a battered sofa. He took an armchair opposite. He steepled his fingers and gave a stagey little sigh. "I was worried about Jessica's schoolwork. She used to be such a brilliant pupil. I thought if I took her out for a quiet meal somewhere, I could find out why her work had been falling off."

239

"Did you call for her at her home?"

"Well, no. I thought something in her home life might be to blame. I arranged to meet her on the steps of the abbey in Mircester. She looked much older. She was wearing a lot of make-up and had her hair up."

"And what did you find out when you weren't complaining about the wine?" asked Patrick.

He flushed angrily. "I had every reason to complain. I know my wines. I have a very good palate."

Agatha and Patrick looked pointedly at the beer cans on the table. "It's a ridiculously pretentious restaurant."

"Does your head teacher know that you were allowing a pupil to drink wine?"

"It was only one glass. I mean, *children* drink wine in France."

"This is not France."

He stood up. "Get out of here, you moralizing old bag."

Agatha stood up as well and her hip gave a nasty twinge. Old, indeed. Her face flamed with anger.

She stalked out followed by Patrick. "Why didn't you ask him more questions?" asked Patrick. "I mean, he might have known more about her affair with Burt."

"Jessica wasn't having an affair with Burt. She was a virgin, remember?"

Agatha pulled out her phone. "Who are you calling?"

"The police."

"We won't operate very well as a detective agency if you keep handing over every lead we have to the police."

But Owen had called Agatha old and she was out for revenge. Bill Wong wasn't there, so she asked for Wilkes. For once he sounded pleased with her.

"Excellent," he said. "We'll get on to it right away."

Agatha told Patrick they should take the rest of the weekend off and start again on Monday. Patrick's normally lugubrious face looked even more disapproving than usual.

"I'll still try to see what I can find," he said.

Agatha went home and entered her cottage. There was no sign of Charles. She went up to the spare room. His bag was gone.

She trailed downstairs in the morning feeling lonely. She went out into the garden, followed by her cats, and sat down. The day had so far been showery, but now puffy white clouds raced across a sky of washed-out blue. The leaves on the trees were already turning a darker green. All too soon it would be the longest day and then the nights would start drawing in, reminding Agatha of her age and the passing of time. She went through to her office and began working on the notes on her computer.

A ring at the front doorbell roused her from her gloomy thoughts. It was Mrs. Bloxby. "I called round to find out how your cases were going," she said.

"Come in," said Agatha, glad of the company. "We can go into the garden."

"Where is Charles?" asked Mrs. Bloxby, looking around.

"He saw some girl from the office window and went scuttling off. His bag's gone."

"He'll be back. He comes and goes. So what has been happening?"

"It's all very complicated. There are three murders and I feel they are entwined in some way."

"Tell me all about it from the beginning."

"Would you like coffee?"

"No, I would like a sherry. I am feeling tired."

"Here! Sit down at the garden table and I'll get you a sherry." Agatha looked at her anxiously. "You do too much. Can't you leave the parishioners to get on without you until you get a rest?"

"Maybe." Mrs. Bloxby leaned back in her chair and raised her face to the sun.

Agatha came back with a decanter of sherry and two glasses. "You don't usually drink."

"This is a special occasion."

"What's that?" asked Agatha, pouring two glasses.

"I rarely take time off from my duties. But this is one of those times. Go on, tell me all about it."

"You know a lot of it already," said Agatha, "but I'll begin at the beginning.

Mrs. Bloxby sipped her sherry and listened intently.

When Agatha had at last finished, she asked, "Did you ever read Kipling?"

"No. What's that got to do with anything?"

"He wrote: 'When the Himalayan peasant meets the he-bear in his pride/He shouts to scare the monster, who will often turn aside,/But the she-bear thus accosted rends the peasant tooth and nail/ For the female of the species is more deadly than the male.' "

"I've heard the last bit. I didn't know it was Kipling."

"Oh, the man's full of quotations. You see, you said that Trixie and Fairy were bullying Jessica. She was a bright student. Maybe they were jealous and wanted to bring her down to their level. Then it may be that Burt was genuinely in love with Jessica. Surely the fact that she was still a virgin bears that out. But he had been having a fling with Joyce. Joyce could have felt bitter and rejected. Mabel Smedley turns out to be computer-literate. Maybe she found something in her husband's emails showing he was having an affair with Joyce."

"And yet," said Agatha slowly, "I still have a feeling that these murders are all linked."

"You've been thinking too hard. Why don't you take a train up to London and walk about the city or go to a gallery?"

Agatha squinted at her watch. "It's two o'clock and I haven't had lunch."

"You could still make the train."

"I'll do that. Finish your sherry. I'll just run up the stairs and get a few things."

But when Agatha returned to the garden, the vicar's wife was fast asleep.

Agatha slowly lowered herself into a chair next to her. Somehow, she did not have the heart to wake her.

So she sat beside her while the cats climbed on her lap, feeling the peace that Mrs. Bloxby seemed able to exude even when asleep.

Jealousy, mused Agatha. Now there was a thought. She remembered when she had come across her ex-husband, James Lacey, entertaining a blonde in the pub, and how she had thrown a terrible scene. She remembered also how corrosive her jealousy had been, how it had taken her over completely. One murder fuelled by jealousy, she could understand. But three! And what did poor Jessica have to do with Smedley? If there had been any record of him visiting that Web site, then Mabel might have done it in a rage. But Patrick had checked carefully and Smedley had never been one of the subscribers. She wondered what Mabel had said to the police about her computer diploma.

The sun sank lower in the sky and Agatha's stomach rumbled. Mrs. Bloxby let out a snore and Agatha smiled. Nice to know the saintly vicar's wife could make vulgar human sounds.

Mrs. Bloxby snored again, choked and

came suddenly awake and looked around startled. "How long have I been asleep?"

"Couple of hours."

"Mrs. Raisin, you should have awakened me. You've missed your train."

"It's all right. You needed the rest. I'd changed my mind about going to London anyway."

Mrs. Bloxby struggled up. "No, you didn't. You let me sleep out of the kindness of your heart. I feel so much better. I'd better get back. My husband will wonder what's become of me."

Agatha looked at her curiously. "Have you ever been jealous?"

"Oh, many times. It's an ordinary human feeling. But it's when ordinary human feelings run riot that the danger starts. Thank you so much."

When she had gone, Agatha was rummaging in her deep freeze looking for something to microwave when the doorbell rang.

She went to answer it and found Roy Silver standing on the step. "Oh, Aggie," he moaned and burst into tears.

"Come in. What's up?" asked Agatha, shepherding him into the sitting room and pressing him down onto the sofa. She handed him a box of Kleenex and waited patiently and anxiously. Roy at last blew his nose and gulped and said, "I've been fired."

"You! Not possible. What happened?"

"It was all because of that pop group I was representing. I decided to get Gloria Smith of the *Bugle* to do a piece."

"Roy! She's poison!"

"But she took me out for dinner and said she'd always admired me, the way I could cope with some dreadful clients. I thought we were getting friendly."

"Oh dear."

"I told her that the pop group were the worst clients I'd ever had to cope with, about them sniffing coke up their noses, wrecking hotel rooms, seducing teenagers, you name it."

"God!"

"She wrote the lot. Two pages. I denied the whole thing, but she'd taped everything. I'm ruined. You see, despite their weird appearance, I'd sold the story that underneath they were all just regular home boys."

Agatha sat back beside him and thought hard. Eventually, she said, "So they're ruined as well."

"That's it."

"Where are they now?"

"Holed up in the Hilton."

"All right. Let's go and sort this out."

"How?"

"Don't ask."

Two hours later Agatha was facing the Busy Snakes in their suite at the Hilton. To Agatha's relief, the lead singer was relatively sober.

"I am here to save your career," she said. "Are you prepared to listen?"

"Do anythink," he said, scratching his crotch nervously.

"Then this is how we'll play it. I will get the *Daily Mail* to run an exclusive about how you really are all the decent boys you were supposed to be. You will tell a pathetic story about how fame and late nights and tours ruined you, but that you are all going into rehab to show young people how they can come about as well. It's the only way you'll get back in public favour. You must say you owe it all to Roy Silver. How he'd tried so hard to help you."

"We don't want to go in no rehab," said the drummer.

"So what do you do?" snarled Agatha. "Sit on your scrawny bums and watch your fame disappear? No one wants you now."

They stared at her. Then the lead singer

said, "Wait outside."

Agatha went out into the corridor and waited, aware the whole time of Roy fretting in the lounge downstairs. At last the door opened.

"Come in," said the lead singer. "Okay, we'll do it."

Agatha worked like a fury most of that night and all the following day, with a bewildered but grateful Roy helping her as best he could.

She drove back to Carsely on the Tuesday morning after having read with pleasure the huge article in the *Daily Mail*. Roy was hailed by the band as "our saviour" and all about how he had tried time after time to straighten them out, until he had unfortunately given that interview to a newspaper. Roy said he had sacrificed his career and done it deliberately because he could not bear to see such fine young men killing themselves. There was a good photo of Roy and one of the band at the gates of a fashionable rehab.

She felt weary when she let herself in. Doris Simpson, her cleaner, had already fed her cats.

Agatha switched off her phone and went to bed. Murder could wait.

Eleven

Harry Beam had diligently followed Joyce without finding her doing anything sinister or, for that matter, anything interesting. She went to the shops, she went to rent videos, she went to the library and then she spent her evenings indoors.

His disguise consisted simply of glasses and a baseball cap pulled down over his face. Joyce certainly showed no signs of being frightened she was being followed or observed by anyone.

One day, he broke off from following her to drive to Smedleys Electronics, which was now called Jensens Electronics. Like Smedleys, Jensens did not appear to want to use an apostrophe. He saw Berry at the gate. He knew it was Berry by the name tag on his overalls and remembered Agatha describing meeting him. Obviously some of the old staff had got their jobs back. Why had Joyce not applied?

Then it dawned on him that the business had been sold very quickly. Didn't wills take longer to process?

He telephoned Agatha. She said that they had just recently been asking themselves the same question, and Patrick had found out through old police contacts that everything had been in Mabel Smedley's name.

He stood looking at the factory, wondering if Joyce had killed Smedley and if she had done so, what she had done with that milk bottle. Joyce carried a capacious handbag. Maybe she had slipped it in there. She said she had scalded it out and put it in the rubbish, but the police had not been able to find it in the bin in her office or in any of the outside garbage bins.

So, thought Harry, if she had it and took it home, would she keep it? Hardly. All she had to do was drop it in a bin in the city centre. Police would have searched the office thoroughly.

He decided to get back to following Joyce for another couple of days.

Meanwhile, Agatha, Patrick and Phil went over and over their notes. At last Agatha said wearily, "We'll need to go back to the beginning and take it one case at a time. I think I've confused the issue by trying to connect them all up. I think we should talk to Trixie and Fairy again. It's half-term. Let's see if we can find them."

They found them both at Trixie Sommers's home. "They're up in Trixie's room," said Mrs. Sommers nervously. "I'll call them down."

The girls sidled into the living room. "Sit down," snapped Agatha. "We've got a few more questions for you."

"Got better things to do," said Fairy.

Mrs. Sommers cracked. "Answer the woman's questions, damn it!" she yelled.

The pair looked shocked and sat down and stared at Agatha, Patrick and Phil with mutinous expressions.

"Now," said Agatha, "you both knew she was romantically involved with Burt. Were you jealous of her?"

"Naah," drawled Fairy. "She was so wet — Burt this, Burt that. How they was going to get married. Carried her engagement ring on a chain round her neck."

Agatha stiffened. She remembered Jessica's body clearly. There had been no chain round her neck with any ring.

"It wasn't on her body when she was found."

"Then whoever killed her nicked it," said Trixie. "Can we go?"

"No, stay where you are," ordered

Agatha. "If Burt loved her, how did he inveigle her into posing for that Web site?"

"Told her it was just a bit of fun, nothing really dirty, and we'd all make money. She'd have done anything for him."

"Did Jessica know Burt had already done time for armed robbery?"

"None of us knew," said Fairy. "Cool."

"Did you know that Jessica had at least one evening out with your maths teacher?"

"Yeah," said Trixie. "Like she told us. Said he was an awful old ponce, bitching about the wine and trying to get into her knickers."

"And you didn't think to tell the police?"

"Don't tell the fuzz everything."

"Look, if you know anything at all, you should tell us. We know Burt had an affair with Joyce Wilson, the secretary at Smedleys. Did Jessica know about that?"

"Don't think so."

"Did you ever see him with any other woman?"

"No, but he had a reputation around the factory as a ladykiller. We told Jessica to get him to have a test before she let him get his leg over," said Trixie. "I mean, these days, you never know where they've been."

Oh, the innocence of youth! Where has it gone? wondered Agatha.

"Is that the lot?" asked Trixie.

"I suppose so," said Agatha, feeling defeated. Not only was she never going to solve Jessica's murder, she thought wearily, but her investigations on the other two were going nowhere as well.

Harry was about to give up watching Joyce, but then, towards evening, she emerged from her house and got into a taxi. He ran to the end of the street where he had parked his motorbike and set out in pursuit. He followed the cab out along the Fosse until it turned off down a country lane. She's going to Ancombe, thought Harry. Maybe a break at last.

The cab went straight to Mabel Smedley's house — or what Harry assumed must be Mabel's house. He thrust his bike into some bushes and waited until the cab had left and wondered how to get near the house without being seen. He shinned over the garden wall and crept through the shrubbery. There was a short tarmac drive up to the house, but it was bordered on either side with yew and laurel.

He eased closer to the house and parted the branches of a laurel bush. Both women were standing in the living room. There were no curtains at the window. He was to wonder later why the significance of that small detail didn't mean more to him at the time. They were talking seriously. He wished he could hear what they were saying. Then they both rose and came out of the house and got into Mabel's car. He hurried back to where he had left his motorbike. Agatha and Phil had told him how Mabel had spotted them following her to the cinema. He'd need to be careful.

He shrank into the bushes by his motorbike as Mabel's car roared past. He got on his bike and followed after waiting impatiently. There were two roads out of the village. One led to Carsely and the other to the Fosse. He dared not get close enough to see which one they took and opted for the Fosse.

Sure enough, when he reached the top of the road and swung out onto the Fosse, he could see Mabel's car ahead in front of two others. He followed at a careful distance. Mabel swung off before the place where Jessica's body had been found. He realized she was taking Joyce home. Sure enough, she dropped Joyce at her house and then drove off again.

Phil phoned Mabel later that evening. "We didn't make another arrangement," he said. "I would like to see you again."

"How nice," said Mabel. "I'm pretty tied up this week. What about next Tuesday? We could have lunch."

"Excellent," said Phil. "I'll pick you up at twelve-thirty and take you somewhere nice."

Bill Wong called on Agatha that evening. She told him about the missing engagement ring. Bill gave an exclamation of annoyance. "You should have told me right away. Wait until I phone this information in."

Agatha waited until he had finished. "I haven't seen the pathology report," said Bill. "We'll need to ask the pathologist if there was any sign of a chain being ripped from her neck. We'll also need to send men back out to the murder site to comb the area and look for that ring. Then we'll need to check all the jewellers in case someone tried to sell it."

"What did Mabel say when confronted about that diploma?"

"She insists that all she learned were the basic skills of computing and the college bears that out. She said that when we first asked her and she said that she knew nothing about computers, she thought they meant was she expert in computing."

"Sounds like a load of cobblers," said Agatha cynically. "There's someone at the door. Wait a minute."

She came back followed by Harry. "Bill, Harry's been following Joyce. He says that earlier today she took a cab to Mabel's, the two women talked and then Mabel ran Joyce home."

"Interesting," said Bill. "But maybe innocent. After all, Mabel would know Joyce from the business."

"But why would she want to talk to the girl her husband had been having an affair with?"

"I'm sure she'll have some perfectly innocent explanation."

"That one always has some perfectly innocent explanation."

"What I'm interested in," said Harry, "is that milk bottle. The missing one. Say Joyce popped it in her handbag. I'm sure the police didn't search it. Or maybe there was somewhere in her little office where she hid it."

"The police searched everywhere."

"If only I could get inside that office and have a look around," said Harry.

"Don't!" ordered Bill. "I've had enough of your unorthodox methods."

"Jealousy," said Agatha suddenly. "And

blackmail. Have you found that teller who took the deposit yet?"

"Yes, she said a rather scruffy man deposited the money on both occasions."

"What about the security tapes at the bank?"

"We were too late getting to them. The ones for the dates of the deposits had been reused."

"Let me see," said Agatha. "Burt had been having an affair with Joyce. He knew about Joyce's affair with Smedley. Say he threatened to tell Mabel. It turns out everything was in Mabel's name. She could have sold the business from under him. It's a wonder *he* didn't murder *her.* And why was everything in her name? I got the impression she was a bullied wife."

"Evidently she has a great deal of money of her own. She was the one who funded the business to get it started on the understanding that everything was kept in her name. And if Smedley was being blackmailed, then he could have paid someone to deposit the money."

Harry sat lost in thought. He had hit upon a plan to get into that office.

The next day, Phil phoned in and said he was feeling poorly and would like the day off. What he really wanted to do more than anything was to call on Mabel. After a lot of thought, he had decided that there was surely an innocent explanation for that diploma. He was beginning to fantasize about marrying Mabel. He was years older than she was, but he was sure she was not indifferent to him.

Patrick had left early for the office, so he did not have to pretend to be sick. Phil decided to walk the two and a half miles to Ancombe.

The day was fine but unseasonably chilly, all the sunny promise of that glorious spring having disappeared. Perhaps he might run into her in the village. When he got to Ancombe, he went into the village shop in the hope that she might be there. Then he remembered she often did the flowers at the church, but the church was empty.

Surely it would be all right just to call at her home. They were friends, after all. He walked to Mabel's home and rang the bell. There was no reply, but he could smell smoke coming from the back garden.

He walked around to the back of the house. Mabel was standing over an oil drum from which black smoke was pouring. Something made him retreat to the corner of the house, put his head round and watch. She went back into the house and shortly afterwards came back out with a pile of video cassettes. She threw them into the drum and poured what looked like petrol on top of them. She stared down into the drum and then gave an exclamation of annoyance and went back into the house.

Gone for matches, thought Phil. He never knew later what prompted his next action but he nipped across the back garden and seized one of the videos out of the drum and scampered back to the shelter of the house just as Mabel reappeared with a box of matches. She struck a match and threw it into the drum and backed away as the contents went up in a sheet of flame.

Phil hurried off. By the time he reached home, he had a stitch in his side and was feeling his age.

He went into his house and took out the video, which he had stuffed in the poacher's pocket of his waxed coat. Then he smiled. "Well, I'll be damned. *Brief Encounter.* That's the film Harry took Joyce to see," he said aloud. Mabel must be cleaning out the house. But then he wondered why such a do-gooder as Mabel had not sent her videos to a church sale or to some old folks' club.

May as well see it anyway, he thought. I'm supposed to be ill. Funny how some people still have video cassettes. I thought everyone had DVDs these days.

He dug out his old video recorder, glad he hadn't thrown it away, fixed it up and slotted the video in.

He leaned back in his armchair. Then he sat up straight and gazed at the screen in horror.

He fumbled for the phone and dialled Agatha. "You'd better come to my cottage immediately," he said in a quavering voice. "There's something you've got to see."

Agatha and Patrick eventually arrived to find Phil looking white and shaken. "You really do look ill," said Agatha.

"It's not that. I went to see Mabel. She was burning videos in her back garden and didn't see me. I don't know why, but when she went indoors to get matches, I stole this one. Look!"

They stared at the screen. Jessica, Trixie and Fairy were cavorting on what they now knew to be Burt Haviland's bed.

"It was in a *Brief Encounter* container," said Phil. "But there must be some innocent explanation. She might not know what was really in there."

"Oh, she did," said Agatha. "Deep down, although you may not know it, Phil, you never really trusted her, or you wouldn't have behaved the way you did."

"I thought I adored her," said Phil in a low voice.

"Anyway," said Patrick, "we'd better tell the police."

"Not yet," said Agatha. "She'll plead innocence and that will be that. Mrs. Bloxby said she thought jealousy held the whole thing together. This Burt seems to have been prepared to lay anything in sight. Oh, yes, he does seem to have been in love with Jessica, although he had a strange way of showing it. What if . . . I mean, just what if Burt had indulged in an affair with Mabel? He must have seen her around often enough. What if two jilted women had it in for Burt? Burt may have supplied Smedley with those videos. Mabel found them and that added to her hatred of both Burt and her husband and Jessica. Do you still have those photographs of Mabel, Phil?"

"Yes, of course," said Phil, thinking sadly of how many times he had taken them out and looked at them. He still couldn't believe his behaviour in stealing that video but came to the conclusion that ever since he had found that diploma, somewhere inside him he had begun to mistrust her.

"The plan is this," said Agatha. "We'll all need photos of Mabel and Burt and we'll go around every hotel and restaurant in the whole area to see whether they've ever been seen together. Maybe that's why Smedley wanted his wife followed. Burt may have been blackmailing him and he may have suspected his wife was close to Burt.

"I'll phone Harry and get him on to it as well." But there was no reply to Harry's phone.

Harry, who had found out the name of the new owner-manager, presented himself at the front desk of Jensens Electronics, gave the fictitious name of John Macleod, and said he had an appointment with Mr. Jensen.

The receptionist picked up the phone and talked into it. Then she said to Harry, "Mr. Jensen's secretary says she has no record of any appointment, and furthermore Mr. Jensen is absent on business, so he has no appointments for today."

"There must be a misunderstanding," said Harry. "May I talk to her?"

The receptionist picked up the phone again. Then she replaced the receiver when she had finished talking and said, "Take a seat. Miss Morrison will be out in a moment."

Harry had hoped for some girl he could charm, but Miss Morrison turned out to be middle-aged, Scottish, and with a brisk no-nonsense manner.

"Mr. Macleod? You're wasting your time, young man."

"But I have a letter here from Mr. Jensen himself!"

The rubbish bins from the firm had been placed out on the road the night before for collection in the morning. Harry had rummaged through them until he found a letter which had not been shredded. He had carefully copied the letterhead on his computer and then had written a letter supposed to be from Mr. George Jensen saying he was impressed by his qualifications and asking him to call at eleven-thirty that day.

Miss Morrison read the letter with raised eyebrows. "He said nothing of this to me. Follow me, young man."

Harry followed her through to her office. "Take a seat," she ordered. "I'm just going to check the boss's appointment book."

Harry looked quickly around. Two filing

cases, desk and computer, one typing chair and one for visitors. A large cheese plant. There was a small kitchen off the secretary's room with a sink and a coffee machine beside it.

He did not have time for anything but a quick look, because she came back in and said, "There's nothing in his appointment book. Leave your number and I'll phone you when he gets back."

Harry got to his feet and thanked her. He looked at the cheese plant. "Fine specimen you've got there," he said, playing for time, hoping to engage her in some sort of conversation so that he could have a better look at the office.

"Oh, that," she said with a dismissive snort. "Wouldn't like it, would you? The last people left it. It blocks out the light from the window."

"No," said Harry, "you're welcome to it. Not going to be a very nice summer by the looks of things."

"Off with you. I haven't got time to chat here all day. I'll phone you. What's that number?"

Harry made up a phone number for her and then left.

He stood outside the gate, his brain busy. He thought about that cheese plant.

Could the police possibly have missed it? Could Joyce have dug a hole at the base of the plant and put the milk bottle in there? And if she had, wouldn't she have dug it up again when things had calmed down and got rid of it?

Harry decided to try to see Bill Wong and put the idea to him. He got on his motorbike and went to police headquarters, only to be told that Bill was out.

He retreated to a café across the parking lot in front of the building where he could watch the comings and goings. He took off the baseball cap and the glasses. Bill would ask how he knew about the cheese plant. But he remembered from all the notes that Agatha had been in that office with Charles, asking Joyce for addresses.

He took out his mobile and phoned Charles. Unlike Agatha's usual phone calls, where she was blocked by either Gustav or the aunt, Charles himself answered the phone.

"When you were in Joyce's office," asked Harry, "was there a cheese plant there?"

"Can't remember. Why?"

"Nothing. Just checking my notes." A young woman's voice could be heard in the background calling, "Where are you, Charles?"

Poor Agatha, thought Harry, ringing off. Hope she isn't keen on him.

He looked across the square again just in time to see Bill getting out of a car.

Harry ran across the square and accosted him on the steps of police headquarters.

"What are you all smartened up for?" asked Bill crossly. "If Wilkes gets a look at you, he might begin to wonder again about the young man who was seen with Joyce."

"Never mind that. There's a whopping great cheese plant in Joyce's old office in a big pot."

"So?"

"She could have buried a milk bottle in there easy."

"I think someone would have looked. I'll check up on it."

Bill thought hard as he went into the station. He went to see Wilkes. He knew Wilkes would not give the matter much serious thought if he learned it came from what he termed "that stupid amateur agency."

"I've had an idea, sir," began Bill.

"All right, then. Spit it out."

"In Joyce Wilson's office, there was a large cheese plant."

"What's a cheese plant?"

"Great big green thing like a young tree in a large pot. If by any chance Joyce Wilson is guilty, could she have hidden the missing milk bottle in there?"

"A team of forensic experts went over every single thing in that office. Besides, if it's such a monster, the new secretary has probably got rid of it."

"Wouldn't do any harm to phone and ask, sir."

"Look here, we're overloaded with cases. Three murders and a spate of burglaries. Leave it."

Agatha managed to get Harry on his mobile and asked him to join in the search of hotels and restaurants to see if Mabel had ever been spotted with Burt. She said they had left photographs of Mabel and Burt for him at the office.

Phil had received a text message from Mabel cancelling their date but suggesting the week after next. Part of him couldn't help still hoping that there would be an innocent explanation for everything to do with Mabel.

Harry picked up the photographs at the office and stood lost in thought. Where would Mabel and Burt go for a liaison —

that is, if they ever went anywhere together?

He decided to ask his father. His father was a successful architect. Harry's parents' marriage had nearly broken up two years ago when Harry's mother found out that her husband had been having a fling with his secretary.

That evening, Harry went to his parents' home. His father, Jeremy Beam, welcomed him. "Your mother's gone out to her Women's Institute meeting. Still working for that detective agency?"

"Yes, that's why I'm here. If a married woman was having an affair with a young employee of her husband's, which hotel or restaurant around Mircester would they go to?"

"Ouch! Meaning you thought I would know?"

Harry waited in silence.

"Let me think," said his father.

"Oh, for heaven's sake," said Harry. "Where did you take your piece of fluff?"

"Don't get cheeky with me, young man."

"Come on, Dad. It's important."

"Well," said Jeremy huffily, "there's this little country hotel, the Manor, in the village of Tewby Magna."

"Where's Tewby Magna?"

"You take the Mircester bypass as far as the Evesham Road turn; go down there and you'll see the signpost."

Harry set off with high hopes. He'd had such a lot of luck recently that he was almost startled when they told him at the hotel that they had never seen anyone answering the descriptions of Mabel or Burt.

Agatha could not sleep that night. If they did find out that Mabel had been anywhere with Burt, what then? If they told the police, Wilkes would ask what gave them the idea. They would need to turn that tape over to the police before much longer and try to pretend that Phil had just found it.

Her idea, which had seemed so bright and logical, now seemed far-fetched. The trouble was she always thought of Mabel as middle-aged because of her dowdy appearance. But Mabel was comparatively young.

Bill Wong was having a restless night as well. He had questioned the forensic team himself, but two of them were on holiday and one had left and the others couldn't remember if anyone had searched the plant pot.

Agatha, Phil, Patrick and Harry met in the office next morning with lists of where they had been so that one of them didn't make the mistake of going back to an old address.

The trouble was, she thought as she got in her car, that if they had been having an affair, they could simply have gone to Burt's flat. Perhaps it was all a waste of time. Give it one more day.

Harry had come to the same conclusion. He made his way to the block of flats where Burt had lived. He trudged up and down the stairs, knocking at doors, but the building was silent. Everyone must be out at work, he thought. He was just about to give up when he saw a man carrying two shopping bags entering the building.

"I wonder whether you can help me," began Harry. "I work for a detective agency."

"Work for your mother, do you? Her was asking me questions the other week. I'm Burden."

Burden by name and Burden by nature, thought Harry with irritation.

"No," he said patiently, "I am employed by Mrs. Raisin. I have photographs here I would like you to look at to see if you recognize anyone."

"I've forgotten to buy me fags. Can't think without a cigarette."

"I'll get you some. Which is your flat?"

"Number eight."

"What do you smoke?"

"Rothmans. Get me a carton."

Greedy old sod, thought Harry, but he ran to the corner store and bought a carton.

"Now," he said when he handed the cigarettes over, trying not to look accusingly at the cheap roll-up which was dangling from Mr. Burden's mouth, "have a look."

"Fix us a cup of tea first."

Harry went through to the kitchen. The sink was full of greasy unwashed dishes. He searched around until he found a clean mug.

"Make it strong," came the order from the living room. Harry put two tea bags in the mug and dunked them until the tea was almost black. "Milk and sugar?" he called.

"Five lumps and the milk's in the fridge."

Harry carried the mug through to him and then opened the folder of photographs, selecting the ones of Mabel.

"Ever seen this woman before?"

He waited patiently while Mr. Burden greedily tore open the carton of cigarettes, selected a packet, opened it, extracted a cigarette, crushed out his roll-up, put the fresh cigarette in his mouth and lit it. He took a swig of tea and said, "Okay. Let's see."

He scowled horribly down at the photographs and then his face cleared. "Oh, her."

"You've seen her?"

Harry could hardly contain his excitement.

"I saw her from the window. Middle o' the night, it were. Can't sleep. My prostate. Pee, pee, pee all night long. The doctor says —"

"But you saw her," Harry interrupted.

"She was getting in a car and that murdered chap was standing there and she was shouting something at him. I recognize her 'cos she was plain, not like the birds he usually had up there."

"How long before the murder?"

"Can't think. Maybe a week."

"Did you tell the police?"

"Naw. They was asking about people calling the night o' the murder."

"Thank you very much, Mr. Burden."

"Wouldn't like to wait a bit, young fellow? I go down to the pub at eleven."

"Got to go."

Bill Wong had decided to risk Wilkes's wrath and go to Jensens Electronics late afternoon on the following day. He didn't think they would demand a search warrant. He was told to wait and then was confronted by Miss Morrison, who raised her eyebrows when he said he wanted to examine the cheese plant in her office.

"Don't take all day about it," she said. "I've got work to do."

Bill followed her through to the office where the cheese plant in all its greenery loomed up against the window. He took out a thin metal rod. "I'll try not to destroy it."

"Won't bother me," said Miss Morrison. "I hate the thing."

Bill crouched down by the pot and slid the rod into the earth. He hit something hard. Maybe it was just the bottom of the pot or there were stones in the bottom.

He pulled a garbage bag out of his pocket, took out a trowel from another pocket and began to scoop the earth into the bag. He scooped and scooped, occasionally changing his tactics to scrape away the soil. Deep down in the pot he saw a gleam of glass. He gently scraped and scraped until a milk bottle was partly uncovered.

God bless Harry Beam, he thought. He took out his phone and called Wilkes.

Agatha, Patrick, Harry and Phil met at her cottage. "Right," said Agatha. "I suggest we go tomorrow morning and confront Mabel with what we've got."

"I think we should tell the police," said Patrick.

"We've found out things they couldn't," said Agatha. "Let's see her first and then talk to them.

They set out for Ancombe the next morning. Harry wondered whether to tell Agatha about his theory about the milk bottle but decided against it. She might be angry with him for telling the police and not her.

Patrick and Phil were in Agatha's car and Harry followed on his motorbike.

The drive outside Mabel's home was empty. Her car was gone.

"We'll wait for her," said Agatha.

"You know," said Patrick, getting out of the car, "that house has an awfully empty look."

He walked up to the windows and peered in. He turned round. "Everything's gone," he said. "All the furniture. Everything."

"She must have sold the house and moved."

"The 'For Sale' sign is still up," said Agatha, "and believe me, if it had been sold, then the estate agents would have a big 'Sold' sign. We'd better tell the police."

She rang and was told that neither Bill Wong nor Wilkes was available, but they would pass on a message. So Agatha left an urgent message that they thought Mabel Smedley might have disappeared. She said they were outside Mabel's house and would wait until someone arrived.

The police had just finished searching Joyce's house again. Bill had pressed to have it searched the previous evening, but it had been late by the time he got hold of Wilkes and Wilkes had said they should organize a team for the morning. There was no sign of her, and although all her furniture was still in place, it looked as if some of her clothes were missing.

Bill got the call from headquarters that Agatha was at Mabel Smedley's house and that she appeared to have sold or stored all the contents and fled.

Wilkes, Bill Wong and a police officer raced over to Ancombe.

"What put you on to her?" asked Wilkes. "As you are all here, I assume it wasn't a social call."

Agatha handed him the video. "Phil originally came to call on her — they were friends — and he found this in the back garden beside a drum full of burnt stuff. He took it home and looked at it and found it was a video of the girls' Web site. Phil didn't look in the windows, he had merely gone round to the back garden in case she was there, so he told us and we all came round to see what she had to say about it."

"You should have phoned me right away!" raged Wilkes.

"It wouldn't have made any difference," said Agatha defiantly. "She'd already have been gone. What about Joyce? Burden told Harry he'd seen them together."

"Joyce has gone as well," said Bill. "We found the missing milk bottle at last. It was buried in a cheese-plant pot in the secretary's office. Some of the old staff are working for the new employers. Maybe Miss Morrison talked about my visit yesterday and one of them phoned Joyce."

Wilkes took out his phone. "I'll get an alert out to watch all airports and ports and railway stations. What was the number of Mrs. Smedley's car?"

"I have it," said Phil, taking out a notebook. He read it out to Wilkes, who phoned in the alert.

"We'll get a team out here to search the house," said Wilkes when he had rung off, "and you lot are coming back to the station. I want statements from all of you. The secretary at Jensens said some young man called about a fictitious appointment. I want to know if that visit had anything to do with you lot."

Back in an interview room, Wilkes switched on a tape and said grimly, "Now, Mrs. Raisin, begin at the beginning. You obviously suspected Mabel Smedley, otherwise Mr. Phil Witherspoon would not have decided to examine a videotape that looked like *Brief Encounter*."

"I was going to come and see you today anyway," said Agatha. "Harry found out last night that Mabel had been seen outside Burt's flat having a row with him. I began to think that somehow the murders were all tied up together. I thought if Burt had been having an affair with Mabel as well as Joyce, but was determined to marry

Jessica, jealousy might have been the motive. Now I think that maybe Mabel and Joyce joined forces. Mabel had a controlling and bullying husband. He could have his affairs, but he wasn't going to allow her any, and I think he may have suspected Burt, so he employed us to watch his wife. Mabel found those videos of Jessica and that added fuel to the fire. I think that explains why Jessica's murder was not sexual. One of them killed her."

"We can understand now why Joyce Wilson fled," said Wilkes, "but why Mrs. Smedley? We really had no proof she had done anything."

"I think she planned all along to get away in case you found something," said Agatha. "She had time to get the contents of her house put into storage, which is what she must have done. You can't blame us for her getting away."

The questioning went on all day and they were all weary by the time they gathered in Agatha's office that evening.

"I didn't tell them about the milk bottle," said Harry. "It wasn't Bill who interviewed me, it was another detective who kept breaking off the questioning to tell me how much he detested amateurs and to get a real job."

"Where could they have gone?" fretted Agatha.

"Anywhere," said Patrick gloomily.

"I wonder if Joyce is calling the shots," said Agatha. "Joyce hadn't money, but according to young Harry here, she was greedy. She may have forced Mabel to run, saying if she didn't help her, she would be forced to betray her. Wait a bit. Joyce wouldn't want to hole up in the north of Scotland or the mountains of Wales. She'd like a bit of luxury. Harry, did you recognize any of the old staff?"

"I don't know any of them. Oh, that security man, Berry, was on the gate. I saw his name tag."

"We'll start with him," said Agatha. "He'll be home by now."

Berry was watching a football match on television and looked irritated at being interrupted.

"What we wondered," said Agatha, "is if any of the same staff are still working there that Joyce may have gossiped with in the past."

"There's Mary Penth. They was close. I remember her saying she rented a room near Joyce's house."

Agatha and Patrick hurried off. They

went to the street where Joyce had lived and began to search along the houses on either side. Unlike Joyce's, they had been divided into flats. "Here it is," said Patrick at last. "Top floor. Mary Penth." He rang the bell.

They heard a clatter of heels and then a young woman opened the door. She was small and neat with sandy hair and tight little features.

Agatha took a deep breath, introduced themselves and explained why they had called, while Mary put her hand to her mouth and let out little whimpers of surprise. "You'd better come in," she said faintly.

They followed her up a steep staircase to the top of the house. "It's my studio," she said, ushering them in. Studio, reflected Agatha, was a real estate agent's name for one room with a kitchen and a minuscule shower tacked on.

"Would you like tea or coffee?" asked Mary.

"No," said Agatha. "What I would really like to know is if Joyce ever talked about a place abroad or somewhere where she would really like to live."

She frowned. "I'm trying to think. I can't really believe Joyce would murder anyone. We had such laughs. I phoned her yesterday. I told her, 'You'll never guess the excitement. They've found a milk bottle in that cheese plant.' I saw no harm in telling her. We were such friends. I couldn't believe for a moment she had done anything wrong."

"Did you know she was having an affair with Robert Smedley?"

"No! Surely not. In fact, I used to tease her about not having any boyfriends."

"Did you never wonder how she was able to rent a whole house?"

"She said she had rich parents. Oh dear. She must have been lying to me all along."

"Did she ever go abroad on holiday?"

"Just the once and only for a weekend. Let me think. She said Daddy was taking her to Marbella."

"Daddy was probably Robert Smedley."

"Joyce went on about how beautiful it was and how she'd like to live there."

Agatha was suddenly anxious to be off. They thanked Mary and made their way out.

"Let's go home and pack," said Agatha. "I'll tell Phil and Harry to hold the fort."

Twelve

Mabel drove steadily and competently down through Spain. She was feeling tired and depressed. She had meant to get clean away on her own. She had put all the furniture in storage and had transferred her money to an offshore account in the Cayman Islands.

And then Joyce had come round to say that the milk bottle had been found and unless Mabel helped her escape, she would tell the police everything. She began to call the shots, saying she wanted to go to Marbella. Mabel pointed out that Spain no longer harboured British criminals, and if found, they could be extradited, but Joyce was adamant. Mabel felt it was all a dreadful mistake. If she hadn't been so flustered and frightened and on her own, she would have hidden out in London under an assumed name and tried to find out how to get a forged passport. Mabel planned to stay in Marbella for one night to shut Joyce up and then move on.

Mabel had abandoned her car in the south of England and had paid cash for a new Land Rover.

Once in Marbella, she would find some way to get rid of Joyce. Mabel loathed Joyce, but she had joined forces with her, motivated by one great hate: Mabel was desperate to rid herself of the husband she had once loved so much. It had not crossed her mind until much later that he had married her only for her money. At first she had admired the way he had set up the electronics business, and saw him as a captain of industry. But gradually he had turned surly, possessive and bullying. Mabel soon discovered that he was possessive, not through love, but because he feared she would take her money away from him if she found someone else. When she met Burt, it was as if all her old girlhood dreams had come true. She had been so sure that Burt was in love with her, but when she began to talk of divorcing Robert, Burt had told her about Jessica. Jealous Joyce had been watching Burt's flat and had known of the affair. She had called on Mabel and Mabel was at first delighted to share her pain with another betrayed woman. At first she had decided to divorce Robert. He had given her a beating and said he would kill her.

And then she had found those videos. Her jealousy of Jessica had become corrosive. She began to stalk her. That was how she knew when the girl went to the nightclub. Girls were always getting murdered on the road home from nightclubs, or so she told herself. She waited until she saw Jessica leave the club. If the girl had been with friends, Mabel would have abandoned the idea. But she raced ahead and waited a little along the bypass until she saw Jessica appear, and drove quickly up. She introduced herself and said, "What is a young girl like you doing out at this time of night?" Jessica had said she was going home from the club. "Where's home?" Mabel asked, just as if she didn't know. When Jessica told her, Mabel said, "Hop in. I'll drive you there." And the trusting Jessica did.

It was when Jessica started saying, "This isn't the road home," that Mabel had pulled the car over to the verge, taken a knife out of her handbag, and stabbed her in the chest. She waited patiently until the girl died and then, when the road was clear, pulled her out of the car and rolled her body down from the verge and dragged it up into the woods.

She ripped Jessica's knickers off, hoping the police might think it a sex crime. Then she saw the ring on the chain round Jessica's neck, an engagement ring, and tore it off the girl's dead body in a fury.

Two days later, she took the dagger out of its hiding place in her kitchen and decided to bury it in the garden. Robert appeared behind her. He looked down at the knife and said, "You killed Jessica."

She had stared at him in terror. Then he had said if she did not sign the firm and all the money and the house over to him, he would go to the police. She promised. What else could she do?

That was when she decided to enlist Joyce's help, saying that when the fuss died down she would pay her a quarter of a million pounds. She had been alarmed when she had found Robert had hired a detective agency and told him he'd better call them off or she would not sign anything.

Joyce, beside her in the passenger seat, remembered how she had said she wouldn't do it. That was until that weekend in Bath, when Robert had calmly told her he had no intention of divorcing his wife.

At first, after the murder, she couldn't believe her luck. She was sure the police would search the plant and cursed herself for not having got the milk bottle out of the office somehow. But when she had got back into the office, she somehow couldn't bear to dig up that milk bottle. The police hadn't found it. Better to leave it where it was, that's what she had thought. What a fool she'd been!

And then, just when things looked as if they were settling down, Burt had called on Mabel and blackmailed her, saying he would tell the police about his affairs with her and with Joyce. He said he was sure one of them had killed Jessica.

In a panic, they had gone together to his flat and murdered him.

Joyce turned plans over in her head. Why shouldn't she have all Mabel's money herself? Mabel was carrying a great deal in cash just in case the police somehow managed to freeze that account in the Cayman Islands. Maybe it would be better to get rid of Mabel, some sort of accident, or something that looked like food poisoning.

Agatha and Patrick left on an Iberian Airline flight to Marbella the next morning. Patrick volunteered he had never been abroad before. Agatha wondered, as she had done before, what the flirtatious Miss

Simms had ever seen in the retired detective with his lugubrious face and thinning hair. He was wearing a dark suit, striped tie, and highly polished black shoes. Agatha thought that, however retired, Patrick's whole appearance screamed copper.

"I hope you brought some light clothes," said Agatha. "It's going to be hot down there. I'm going to study this guidebook and try to figure out where they might be. I think Joyce would want a beach, but there are so many — Casa Blanca beach, La Fontanilla beach, El Faro beach — oh, here's something. Nagueles beach. It says here it's situated on the Golden Mile of Marbella. There's the Hotel Puente Romano and the Hotel Marbella Club. Sounds just like the sort of places Joyce would like unless Mabel has persuaded her to hide in a pension in the backstreets."

"I'm worrying about this," said Patrick. "Surely Mabel won't just go where Joyce wants her to go."

"Maybe she has to. Maybe Joyce is threatening to go to the police. I mean, Mabel may be guilty of all the murders, with Joyce just being an accessory."

"Let me see that guidebook," said Patrick.

He flicked through it. "It's such a big

place," he mourned.

"We've got to try," said Agatha.

"If you say so. But they'll have Interpol on to it by now."

"But they don't know about Spain, and we do."

Joyce stepped out on the balcony of their hotel and took a deep breath of sunny air. A golden beach stretched out in front of a green-blue sea. A young man was strolling along the promenade. He looked up and saw Joyce on the second-floor balcony and blew her a kiss.

Joyce's spirits soared. This was the life! She went back into the suite and said excitedly, "It is so beautiful here. We can go out clubbing tonight."

Mabel looked up from her unpacking. "No, we can't," she said in a flat voice. "You've pushed me too far, Joyce. We will stay in our suite and have our meals sent up until I figure out where we should go that's safer."

"They'll never find us here. Thanks to the European Union, we didn't even get our passports stamped."

"Some border guard might remember us. Marbella is still a thieves' kitchen. They might think of here."

"But that's only for train robbers and big-time crooks. We're only . . ."

"A couple of murderers. Now shut up and let me think."

Joyce studied Mabel for a long moment and then said, "Okay. What about a drink?"

"All right. See what's in the minibar."

Joyce opened it up. "Pretty much everything."

"Fix me something and close those windows and put on the air conditioning. I'm going to splash my face with cold water."

"I'll mix us a couple of Cuba libres," shouted Joyce.

She took out the bottle of rum and two small bottles of Coke and then extracted two tumblers. She went to the bed and rummaged in her bag until she found a bottle of sleeping pills. She split them open with her long lacquered nails and shook the contents into one of the tumblers. Then she poured generous measures of rum into each tumbler and filled both glasses up with Coke.

Just in time. Mabel appeared. "I've been thinking about Brazil. If that train robber, Ronnie Biggs, could hide out there forever, then so can we. I'll have a drink and start making arrangements. You haven't closed the windows."

"Sorry." Joyce handed Mabel her drink and went over and closed them, reluctantly shutting out the splendid view of sun and sea.

Mabel looked down at her drink. There was a small fleck of white powder floating on the top. She quickly switched her drink for Joyce's.

"Here's to us," Mabel said, raising her glass.

"Good luck," said Joyce. "How do we get to Brazil?"

"Dangerous now to fly," said Mabel. "Maybe we'll drive over to Lisbon and see if there's a ship."

Joyce drank eagerly, watching Mabel the whole time for signs of sleepiness. When she felt herself beginning to feel groggy, she could hardly believe it. She stood up and swayed.

"You look tired, dear," said Mabel, steering her through to her bedroom. "Lie down."

Joyce began to struggle. "You switched the glasses."

"You're becoming delirious." Mabel forced Joyce down on the bed. Joyce fought to keep awake, but she was sucked down into blackness.

"That's solved one problem," said

Mabel. She lifted a pillow and was about to press it down on Joyce's face but felt squeamish. She was no longer fuelled by the insane, jealous rage which had turned her into a murderer. She put the pillow down and went back and searched Joyce's handbag. She took out the empty bottle of sleeping pills and threw it in the waste basket. Then she opened Joyce's wallet and took out all the money she had given her. Lying in the bottom of the handbag was an engagement ring. Mabel scowled. She had given it to Joyce to get rid of. She flushed the ring down the toilet and then put the money she had taken out of Joyce's bag into her own. Putting a few belongings into a beach bag, Mabel left the room and hung the "Do Not Disturb" sign on the door. She would have to leave her clothes behind.

She took the lift to the ground floor, found the Land Rover in the car park and drove off, a little smile on her face as she imagined Joyce stranded, without money.

Joyce woke in the evening, feeling groggy and sick. Then memory came flooding back. She struggled out of bed. No sign of Mabel. Joyce saw her own handbag was lying open. She opened her wallet. All her money was gone. Panic set in. What was she going to do?

She decided to go down to the dining room, have a meal and a drink, sign for it and see if food would clear her head.

Joyce was ushered to a table overlooking the sea. A voice said. "What is a pretty lady like you doing dining alone?"

She looked up. A squat little man stood beaming down at her. "Just admiring the sea," said Joyce.

"Mind if I join you?"

"Please do," said Joyce, beginning to see a way out of her predicament. This man was ugly but he looked rich. His suit was well tailored and he wore a heavy gold wristwatch.

If I flirt with him, thought Joyce, then maybe he'll ask me up to his room, and when he's asleep I can take his wallet and maybe his car keys and make a run for it.

"May I introduce myself? I'm Peter Sinclair."

"Do you live here?" asked Joyce.

"No, I own a chain of shoe shops in Britain. I'm over here to check up on my buyers."

Joyce held out her hand. "Ellie Finch," she said. She experienced a sudden cold shock. Mabel had checked them in.

Maybe by now their photographs would be in the British papers and British newspapers were sold in Spain. She'd need to move quickly.

So she began to chat and flirt, but being careful not to drink too much. She would need all her wits about her.

They had started dinner late, at ten o'clock, although that was not very late by Spanish standards. At midnight, Joyce said she would like to retire, giving Peter what she considered her best bedroom look.

"Perhaps you would like to join me in my suite for a nightcap?" said Peter.

Got him, thought Joyce.

Agatha and Patrick were hot and weary. It was their second day of searching. Patrick suggested they return to their own hotel in Marbella for the night and start again in the morning, but Agatha pleaded, "Just a few more hotels. There are two more five stars we haven't tried. Here's one. The Splendide."

Driving carefully in their rented car, and with Patrick navigating, she drove to La Venus beach and parked in front of the Splendide. "Come on, Patrick," said Agatha.

"Agatha, they may not even be here.

This is just another of your wild ideas. I want to go home."

"Just this once."

"It's one in the morning."

"Okay. Wait in the car. I've got the photos."

Agatha trudged into the glittering lounge. The night porter looked superciliously at the middle-aged woman in the crumpled linen trouser suit and said, "Yes?"

Agatha explained who she was and took out the photographs of Mabel and Joyce. "This one," he said, selecting the photograph of Joyce. "I think I saw her leaving the dining room with a Mr. Sinclair."

"Listen!" said Agatha. "These are two murderers wanted by the British police. Call the local police and get them here fast."

The night porter hesitated only for a moment, thinking Agatha might be deranged. Then he gave a mental shrug. The police could deal with it.

Peter Sinclair was struggling with his bonds on the bed and shouting, "You little bitch," as Joyce put his wallet in her handbag.

Being tied up had seemed like an exciting sex game. "Help!" he began to shout.

Joyce glared at him and took a silk scarf out of his wardrobe and stuffed it into his mouth.

She made for the door, but it burst open and she found herself confronted by Spanish police and detectives. Behind them, as in a nightmare, she saw Agatha Raisin.

Patrick woke from a heavy sleep as Agatha got into the car. "Can we go home now?" he asked.

"Soon," said Agatha with a grin. "Joyce has been arrested and she says Mabel is on the road to Lisbon. The Spanish police have alerted the Portuguese authorities."

"And you let me sleep through the whole thing!"

"There wasn't time to wake you. Get the bags out. We're staying here for the night and we've to report to the police station here in the morning."

"How did that bat Raisin do it?" raged Wilkes the following day. "How did she know where to look? She's been withholding information, that's what."

"Without her, I don't think we might have found them," said Bill. "You say Mabel Smedley's been picked up?"

"Before she even reached the Portuguese

border. Joyce Wilson was determined not to suffer alone."

"So what is she saying? Who killed who and why?"

"Burt Haviland had been laying both of them. They were both insane with jealousy of Jessica. Robert Smedley found his wife trying to bury the dagger with which she had killed Jessica in their garden. He told her unless she signed all her money and the business over to him, he would turn her in. So she gave Joyce the weedkiller and told her to get on with it. They killed Burt because he knew something and was threatening to go to the police. They both did that one."

"But that neighbour only heard one set of footsteps leaving Burt's flat."

"That would be Joyce. Mabel's flat shoes probably didn't make a sound."

"Agatha Raisin," said Bill, "often gets results we can't because she doesn't go by the book."

"Then it's time she did," said Wilkes. "It's going to be all over the newspapers tomorrow about how she tracked them down. She'll see to that."

Agatha put down the phone. "Well, that's that, Patrick. Every last British national newspaper. We're to wait here. Their local stringers and photographers are coming here to interview us and take our pictures. We'd better get dressed up."

"I am suitably dressed," said Patrick.

He was wearing a Hawaiian shirt in a pattern of red and yellow, droopy khaki shorts, black ankle socks and open-toed leather sandals.

"It's just that you look so much more the detective in your suit, Patrick, and I've got the air conditioning on. The rest should be here any moment."

"What rest?"

"I told Phil, Harry and Mrs. Freedman to fly out and join us. Don't you see what a good photograph it'll make? The whole of the detective agency."

Patrick sighed and went to change. He wondered where Agatha got all her energy from.

Sir Charles Fraith picked up his copy of the *Daily Telegraph* the following day. He found himself looking at a photograph of Agatha. "Full story pages six and seven," he read. He opened to the relevant pages.

There they all were — Agatha, Patrick, Harry, Phil and even Mrs. Freedman. There were long quotes from Agatha praising the detective abilities of her staff in solving three murders.

Charles felt left out. After all, he had done a lot of unpaid work. But he had to admit that he had left Agatha in the lurch when he went chasing after Laura. And where was Laura? Gone back to her fiancé, that's where. "You didn't even tell me you had a fiancé," he had raged.

"He was abroad," Laura had said. "Don't make a fuss, Charles. We had a nice little fling."

The night before their departure for England, Agatha and her staff celebrated with a lavish dinner in the hotel restaurant. Agatha did not mind the money she was spending. All that publicity would pay dividends. She had carefully told the British press which flight they would all be on when their plane landed at Heathrow. With luck, there would be even more publicity. Of course, now that there was a trial in the offing once the pair were extradited, she hadn't been able to go into all the details.

"Here's to us," said Agatha, raising her glass. "Many more cases, I hope."

"But no more murders," said Mrs. Freedman with a shudder.

"Amen to that," said Phil.

But at first it looked as if there was to be no triumphal homecoming. They were taken from the plane before the other passengers got off and herded into a side room where an angry Wilkes was waiting.

"How did you know they were in Marbella?" he asked Agatha.

"I interviewed a friend of Joyce's who said Joyce had once been in Marbella. It was a long shot."

"You should have phoned me! I could have alerted the police in Marbella and both of them might have been picked up earlier."

"I don't think you would have listened to me," said Agatha. "You would have said something like, 'Run along. We've alerted Interpol.'" Agatha was suddenly very tired. A tear ran down her cheek.

Wilkes was alarmed. If Agatha collapsed on him, the police would be accused of bullying a heroine.

"That's not the case. Run along. We'll contact you later."

He regretted his burst of sympathy when Agatha Raisin produced a large hand mirror from her capacious handbag and began to repair her make-up, ready for any photographers who might be waiting.

Epilogue

Back in Carsely two weeks later on a rainy weekend. Agatha felt very flat. Business was pouring into the agency, but it seemed to be nothing more than the usual lost cats, dogs and teenagers and divorce cases. No kidnapped heiresses and aristocrats wanting their jewels found. Nothing, she thought bitterly, but plod, plod, plod.

Her hip was aching more and more. She phoned up her masseur, Richard Rasdall, and made an appointment for that Saturday afternoon. She felt lonely and deflated after all the excitement. The newspaper interviews and television interviews had dried up.

She looked at the clock and realized she'd forgotten she was supposed to pick Roy Silver up from the train. He had phoned the evening before, asking if he could come on a visit.

She drove down to Moreton-in-Marsh station to find him waiting impatiently in the car park.

"I was just about to phone you," he said.

"Sorry, Roy. I'll leave the car and we'll walk round the corner for a pub lunch. The boss treating you well?"

"With kid gloves, especially considering I am a friend of the famous Agatha Raisin."

"I'm yesterday's news now. I want comfort food. Steak and kidney pie would go down a treat."

Over lunch, she told Roy in detail about solving the murder cases, but she seemed to have told the story so many times that she felt she was beginning to bore herself.

"Did this Mabel Smedley ever say why she employed you to find out who murdered her husband?"

Agatha scowled. "Evidently she told the police I was such an amateur I wouldn't have a hope in hell of finding out anything and employing me would make her look innocent."

"I was surprised not to see Charles in any of the photos."

"Oh, he cleared off well before the end to chase after some floozy. I've got to go to the masseur in Stow. I'll leave you at the cottage. Won't be long."

"I told you before, it does seem to me like a bit of arthritis," said Richard. "I'm not a doctor. Take my advice and get that hip x-rayed."

"It can't be arthritis," raged Agatha. "What do you know?"

"Enough," he said calmly. "But suit yourself."

Once the massage was over, Agatha felt much better. The masseur's treatment room was situated above his chocolate shop, The Honey Pot. Agatha had a sudden sharp longing to reward herself with a big box of handmade chocolates, but marched determinedly out into the square. She stood in the square, irresolute. She felt fine. But why not prove Richard wrong? Agatha had a private doctor, but it was Saturday. Nonetheless, she had his home phone number.

She phoned him and he said he could see her. Hoping for reassurance, her face fell when he said she'd better get the hip x-rayed. Agatha said she wanted to go private, no longer in her worry prepared to wait for the slow-grinding machinery of the National Health Service. He phoned the Cheltenham and Nuffield Hospital and booked her for an appointment with a specialist for Monday evening.

"Where on earth have you been, sweetie?" demanded Roy.

"I had a massage and looked around the shops," lied Agatha.

"Well, you've missed all the excitement. It's on the news. Mabel Smedley's escaped."

"What? From a Spanish jail? How did she do that?"

"She seemed to be having a heart attack and then fell unconscious. They took her to a hospital. The ambulance had to stop for some horrendous crash in front of them on the road there. The ambulance driver and guard got out because to all intents and purposes Mabel was unconscious. She removed all the straps from the stretcher and simply got out and walked away."

"What if she comes after me?" said Agatha, her eyes glowing.

"Aggie, you almost look as if you wish she could."

"Don't be silly."

But for one moment Agatha had envisaged herself catching Mabel and all the circus of publicity coming back to surround her in a warm starry coat that kept the realities of pedestrian life and possible arthritis at bay.

"Put the television on again," she said.

Roy switched on the television set to a twenty-four-hour news channel.

They sat patiently watching trouble in Iraq, an earthquake in Japan, the latest iniquities of the National Health Service, and then there was a news flash. "Mabel Smedley, the British woman wanted for three murders, has just been rearrested by Spanish police. A Spanish police spokesman said she had ordered a drink in a bar and when she walked out without paying for it, the bartender chased her down the street, shouting and yelling. A traffic policeman on duty arrested her. More later."

"I think she wasn't very cunning after all," said Agatha. "I think all the murders were done on impulse, fuelled by sick jealousy, or maybe, in the case of her husband, pure rage. Let's keep watching."

An hour later, Roy said crossly, "Agatha, it's the same thing over and over again. You're not a very good hostess. Let's go and see Mrs. Bloxby. Have you seen her since you got back?"

"No. How awful. Everything's been so busy. Let's go now."

Mrs. Bloxby was delighted to see them and demanded to know all the details. "I can hardly believe Mrs. Smedley capable of such violence and evil," said Mrs. Bloxby when Agatha had finished. "Jealousy really must have turned her mind. You will surely miss that young man, Harry Beam, when he goes to university."

"I'm going to try to persuade him to stay. Patrick is already looking for another detective for me. We're actually short-staffed."

"Jessica's parents must be relieved that the murderer has been caught. What about Joyce? Are her parents alive?"

"It turns out her father was a respectable accountant. Dead these past three years. Her mother is in care in Bath. She has Alzheimer's. Joyce invented a rich father to explain why she was able to rent a whole house."

"The thing that troubles me," said the vicar's wife, "is that I look around our ladies when we meet at the ladies' society and I begin to wonder what strange passions are lurking behind those genteel breasts. I mean, Mrs. Smedley was so admired for her good works and for her gentle manner. Who could ever have guessed she would turn violent? Love is a strange thing and can twist people in so many ways."

Agatha suddenly thought again of her ex-husband, James Lacey. Did he ever think of her? Would he ever come back into her life? And if he ever did, would he find she had turned into some old crock riddled with arthritis? She had been a far from perfect wife, but he had behaved badly towards her and probably never realized it. Most men were protected from admitting their mistakes by a sort of justified selfishness.

Agatha spent a pleasant weekend with Roy and plunged back into work on the Monday, but always thinking of her appointment at the hospital in the evening.

She decided that she would need to employ more than one extra detective. They could not all keep on working in the evenings as well as the days.

At last, she drove reluctantly to the Nuffield Hospital, feeling obscurely guilty at the courteous reception and thinking of all the unfortunate people who could not afford private medicine. She filled in the forms.

"Don't you have health insurance?" asked the receptionist.

Agatha shook her head. She had always believed herself to be immortal.

"Go through to X-ray, along there on

the left," said the receptionist. "The specialist will see you after he receives the X-rays."

Agatha went along to the X-ray department, took off her clothes and put on the gown allocated to her. Then her hips and legs were x-rayed and she was told to get dressed and wait. After a short time, the folder of large X-rays was handed to her and she was told to go back out to the reception area and wait again.

Agatha slid the X-rays out and squinted at them, holding them up to the light, but she could not make out anything.

A nurse approached her and took the X-rays away from her. "Mr. McSporran will see you now. Follow me," she said.

"Are you sure that's his name? Sounds like a Scottish music hall joke."

"McSporran is a good old Scottish name. Please don't make any jokes about it. He does get tired of them."

Mr. McSporran was a small, neat man. He put Agatha's X-rays up on a screen.

"Uh-uh!" he murmured.

"What?" demanded Agatha nervously.

"You will see quite clearly that you have arthritis in your right hip. It is not terribly advanced, but I would advise you to make an appointment for a hip operation. The longer you leave it, the less successful the operation will be."

"I'm too busy at the moment to take time off," said Agatha.

"As I said, it is important you do not leave it too long. We can make arrangements to give you an injection in the hip as a temporary measure. If you are lucky, the injection will last six months."

Agatha felt she had just received a stay of execution. "I'll have it now."

"It doesn't work like that. You will need to make an appointment. You are put under a general anaesthetic. It only takes one day. I would suggest also that you have a bone scan." He opened his diary. "We can do the hip injection for you on the twenty-fifth. That's in two weeks' time. You will need to be here at seven-thirty in the morning and do not eat or drink anything after ten o'clock the evening before.

"All right," said Agatha bleakly.

"Now lie down and let me examine you. Remove your trousers."

Agatha suffered her leg being pulled this way and that.

"Right," he said when he had finished. "Call at the X-ray desk on your road out and make an appointment for a bone scan."

Agatha was just leaving the hospital when her mobile phone rang. It was Charles. "Have you eaten?"

"No, I'm in Cheltenham."

"I'll take you for dinner. I'll meet you in the square in Mircester. How long will you be?"

"The traffic should have thinned out. About three quarters of an hour."

"See you then."

"Why were you in Cheltenham?" asked Charles when they were seated in an Italian restaurant.

"Working on a case," said Agatha, who had no intention of telling Charles about her arthritis. So ageing.

"You've been having a lot of excitement."

"You could have been in on it, Charles, if you hadn't gone scuttling off. How's it going?"

"Turns out she was engaged and was just using me for a bit of a fling."

"Poor you."

"Yes, poor me. Do you ever worry about getting old on your own, Agatha?"

"I hadn't really thought about it."

"Sometimes I think it would be awful to sink into decrepitude on my own."

"You're hardly on your own, Charles. You've got your aunt and Gustav."

"My aunt can't last forever and Gustav is hardly the sort of sympathetic type to soothe the fevered brow. Still, there's always hope. Lots of pretty girls out there."

Agatha obscurely felt she was being dismissed because of her age. Charles was in his forties, but she was only in her fifties. And yet men in their forties could still hope to wed some young miss.

When the meal was over, she hoped Charles would volunteer to stay with her because she did not want to go back to an empty house, but he showed no signs of wanting to. Agatha felt too demoralized to ask him.

She went home alone and checked her phone for messages. There was one from Roy thanking her for the weekend, but the next one made her heart soar. It was Freddy.

"How's my heroine?" he said. "I'll call you at your office tomorrow."

Agatha's black mood lifted. Somebody loved her!

The next day in the office, she jumped whenever the phone rang, waiting for Freddy to call. By late afternoon, she had almost given up hope and was tired of making excuses not to leave the office when he did call. "What about dinner tonight?" he said.

"At what time?"

"I'll pick you up at your cottage at eight."

Without making any more excuses, Agatha left the office and went straight to the nearest hairdresser's. Then, with her hair newly done, she hurried off home to begin elaborate preparations for the evening ahead.

Freddy arrived promptly at eight o'clock and took her to a new restaurant in Moreton-in-Marsh.

Had Agatha not been so elated to be in his company, she would certainly have complained about the meal. Freddy recommended the rolled, stuffed pork belly. When it was served, Agatha found herself staring down at what looked like one small brown turd surrounded by acres of empty plate. It was served with a tiny bowl of mixed salad. But there was handsome Freddy across the table, plying her with questions about the murders and exclaiming in a flattering way at what he described as her brilliant intuition.

And, oh, the way he looked into her eyes

and the way his hand brushed hers as he reached across to fill her wine glass.

They were sitting at a table in the bay of a window. It had started to rain again, but for once Agatha was oblivious to the miseries of the dreary weather.

"Do you know," breathed Freddy, "I fancy you something rotten, old girl."

He should have left the "old" out. Agatha turned away and stared out of the window just in time to see Charles in his car stopping at the pedestrian crossing lights outside the restaurant. He gave her a startled look. The lights changed to green, a car behind him honked and Charles moved on.

Agatha realized Freddy was waiting for some sort of reply, but found she couldn't think of anything that might be suitable come on.

So instead she asked, "How was South Africa?"

"Oh, you know. Same old, same old. Met friends. That sort of thing."

The door of the restaurant opened and Charles breezed in. "Mind if I join you?"

"You weren't invited," snapped Agatha.

"And how are you, Freddy?" asked Charles, ignoring the fact that Agatha was glaring at him.

"Fine," mumbled Freddy.

"Bring the wife and kids back with you?"

"They're still there."

Agatha could hardly believe what Charles was saying.

"When are they joining you?" pursued Charles.

"Next week."

"Jolly good. Well, I better not interrupt your meal. I'll phone you tomorrow, Agatha."

"Wait!" Agatha got to her feet. "I'm coming with you. Give me a lift home. I want to get away from this bastard as quickly as possible."

"I thought you knew I was married," said Freddy.

"How was I to know that when you didn't tell me, and you told that copper right in my kitchen that you weren't married."

"You're a rat, Freddy," said Charles. "Come along, Agatha."

"You should have told me," said Agatha for the umpteenth time when they were both back in Agatha's cottage.

"And you should have told me he had been dating you. How many times do I have to say it?" protested Charles.

"Well, it's all very depressing. I was feeling low as it was. I mean, all that publicity was rather exhilarating, but it suddenly just died away. Midlands TV wanted me for another interview and they cancelled."

"It may have been something to do with Detective Inspector Wilkes."

"What are you talking about?"

"He gave a rather unflattering interview about you in the *Guardian*."

"When?"

"I forget exactly when, but as it happens I've got a copy of the paper in my car. Gustav got it for me."

"If it was unflattering, then he would. Fetch it for me."

Charles went out and came back with a crumpled copy of the *Guardian*.

Agatha riffled through it until she came to the features page. There was a big headline: the inspector and the lucky amateur. She began to read.

Wilkes had been very amusing about Agatha's detective abilities. "I think Mrs. Raisin stumbled on where the murderers were because they were amateurs and she is an amateur," he had said. "She bumbles around my cases like some sort of bumble bee, occasionally, by sheer luck, crashing into the truth. We are grateful to her, of course, but Interpol were on it and they would have been caught eventually." There was a lot more of the same.

"This is character assassination," said Agatha. "I'll sue him."

"I wouldn't do that. Not if you intend to keep running a detective agency. You sue him and you'll soon have the police working against you at every turn."

"You should have told me," protested Agatha. "I could have countered this by reminding everyone it was I who found Jessica's body, not to mention tracking that pair to Spain."

"The paper was old by the time Gustav gave it to me. Anyway," said Charles, "you never mentioned me once in any of your interviews."

"Because you had beetled off chasing a bit of skirt."

"That's it," said Charles. "I'm off. Phone me when you're in a better temper."

Agatha arrived at the office the next morning to find them all waiting for her. "What's this?" she asked wearily. "A strike?"

"We just wanted to be sure that you want to continue with this agency," said Patrick. "You didn't bother doing any work yesterday and you took the whole weekend off."

"Of course I am continuing," said Agatha. "I've just been tired, that's all. Mrs. Freedman, let's go through the work for today."

In order to show enthusiasm, Agatha took on one of the nastier cases, which was following a man whose wife thought he was being unfaithful and wanted grounds for a divorce.

He owned a delicatessen in Mircester. The shop was a popular one. Agatha found a parking place across the road. Phil was beside her with his camera.

Customers came and went. Then the shop was closed for an hour at lunchtime. Their quarry went to a local restaurant but ate on his own.

Back to watching the shop as the hours dragged on until closing time. His two assistants left and then he came out and locked up the shop. He stood outside, looking up and down the street.

"He's waiting for someone," said Agatha, crouching down. "Get ready with the camera. Thank God for the light evenings. Wouldn't want him to be alerted with a flash."

A youngish man came along the street

and hailed the owner. They walked off together.

"Today was a waste of time," said Phil.

"No, get out the car and follow them," said Agatha. "I've got an idea."

They hurried after them at a discreet distance. They stopped outside a club called the Green Parrot.

"Thought so," said Agatha. "Bang off a couple of pictures and let's get out of here."

Phil did as he was told, getting two good shots before the two men walked into the club, their arms around each other's shoulders.

"So why did I have to take photographs?" asked Phil. "Was that his illegitimate son, or what?"

"The Green Parrot is Mircester's only gay club. Sometimes I hate this job. I feel grubby. I'll drive you back to your car, Phil. You can go home now and print up those photos. I just want to look at the books."

After she had left Phil, Agatha slumped down in Mrs. Freedman's chair and stared at the blank computer screen.

She could not remember ever before feeling so old or so lonely. Early fifties surely wasn't old these days. But the fact that she had arthritis had shaken her badly. She envisaged herself crumbling into old age all on her own, no one to look after her, no one to share the pain.

There was a tentative knock at the office door. Agatha was about to shout, "We're closed. Go away," but reflected that business was business and a possible new case might take her mind off her misery.

She opened the door and stared up at the tall figure standing there, smiling down at her.

"Hullo, Agatha," said James Lacey.

About the Author

M. C. Beaton is the author of fifteen previous Agatha Raisin novels, the Hamish Macbeth series, and an Edwardian mystery series written as Marion Chesney. She currently divides her time between the English Cotswolds, where she lives in a village similar to Agatha Raisin's own, and Paris.